Build That Wall

Build That Wall

The Amish Time Traveler book two

With Recipes for Ida Mae's Insect Repellent,
Seven Sweets and Seven Sours
Plus Three Potato Salads

C. K. Stein

To Bob. May you rest in peace.

Cover photo is of an early Mennonite Church in Lower Saxony.

THANK YOU readers from Richland Friends Meeting for their support and comments. To my sister Faith Wyse and Friend Barbara Zucher for their editing. To Tony Lopopolo for helping me learn to write fiction. To Mickey Bernstein and Arlene Stillwater for giving me a reason to write. And to Ann Woolsey, Marie Steciw and all my friends, my children and grandchildren who put up with all the time I've spent reading and writing.

Thank you also to the many readers who bought my books and waited patiently to read the sequel.

Build That Wall

RECIPIES

	Ida Mae's Insect Remedy within text	48
1	German Chocolate Sauerkraut Cake	204
2	Cream Cheese Peanut Butter Frosting	205
3	Funny Cake	206
4	Ground Cherry Pie	207
6	Tapioca Pudding	208
7	Graham Cracker Pudding	209
7	Whoopee Pies	210
8	Grandma B's Oatmeal Coconut Cookies	211
9	Chow Chow	212
10	Three Bean Salad	213
11	End of Garden Pickles	214
12	Green Tomato Pickles	215
13	Bread and Butter Pickles	216
14	Pickled Red Beets	217
15	Pickled Eggs	218
16	Hilde's German Potato Salad	219
17	Aunt Sadie's Potato Salad	220
18	Autumn's Potato Salad	221

ACKNOWLEDGEMENTS

The Second Reich in Muenster Germany

Martin Luther was a devout Catholic priest who sacrificed his health by prayer and constant service to his parishioners. His bishop rewarded him with a trip to the Vatican. Luther came back from his visit to the pope with the feeling of great injustice. He watched his villagers die of starvation and lack of medical care while the pope lived in gluttonous luxury.

In direct rebellion to the pope and supreme ruler of all Europe, Luther translated the New Testament into the common German language in 1552 and followed with the complete Bible in 1534. With the aid of the printing press which had been invented less than 100 years earlier banned copies of Holy Scriptures spread like wildfire. When people read the *written words of Jesus* they rebelled against papal law.

The pope condemned them to death for their heresy but for every dead martyr two more stood up to give their lives in the belief that God would welcome them into paradise for their heroism.

A group of theologians felt as if Luther should go farther from Catholicism. They decided that since John baptized Jesus after he became an adult, all believers should follow his example. These people became known as the Anabaptists. One group of Anabaptists established a new kingdom of heaven on earth based on New Testament theology. They believed that if they lived holy lives they would create the perfect place for Jesus to return on earth. They fortified their walls to keep the unbelievers away and established this kingdom by force. Their leader anointed himself as the new King David who would institute the new kingdom or Reich. It has been suggested that Hitler as well as some communist leaders studied the techniques of the second Reich in order to affect their own political futures.

Many Mennonites and Amish in the USA commemorate the Anabaptist and nonresistant movements in Germany in the sixteenth century. While they remember the martyrs who went before them to pave the way for their beliefs, they may not stress the general knowledge that their founder, Menno Simons', lived during the time of the militant Second Reich or that he opposed it. Menno declared that the Kingdom of God is a peaceable and spiritual realm rather than a worldly domain.

Much has been written about this time in Germany. A good book on the subject is *The Tailor-King* by Anthony Arthur.

Ffernpass

While the Ffernpass Hotel existed in 1985 Austria, the village and events are purely fictional.

Indian Jim's story is based on the memories of a similar event recalled by the plain people of Holmes County Ohio on a much earlier date.

An Italian word such as *mafia* would suggest both a secret and an organized society.

The Amish are a people of few words and they do maintain secrets. They are all accountable to each other and to their elders. Their baptized members do impose strict rules of behavior.

The author finds no evidence of organized patriarchal crime families similar to the flashy Catholics of Mediterranean descent who are called godfathers.

Build That Wall

The Amish Time Traveler

Build That Wall

The Amish Time Traveler

Those who fail to learn from history are doomed to repeat it. Winston Churchill

Those who cannot remember the past are condemned to repeat it. George Santayana philosopher, essayist, poet and novelist. 1863 - 1952

Chapter 1
New Philadelphia Ohio. 1985
Saturday afternoon in July

Kay had left this place as sure as a baby leaves her mother's womb. Sixteen years later she turned her rental car away from the airport onto Route 39 toward Sugar Creek, Ohio.

Maybe she should have just worn shorts. She meant for her modest skirt to show respect for her Amish elders. Should she have bothered? They had never seemed to try to please her.

OAK FURNITURE
by Levi Stoltzfus

The sign read in large black letters over the plain drawing of a wooden rocking chair.

Kay's rented Escort turned into the parking lot on its own.

At least it seemed to.

It stopped in front of the huge store.

In her memories people and places stayed frozen in place.

So much change!

She'd assumed Levi made a new life.

It never felt real before now.

She had left Holmes County at sixteen. Naïve and self-absorbed... she had felt as if she were an adult.

Levi moved on with his life. Pride for him rose in her chest.

She remembered his proposal of marriage and looked for his buggy.

The three pickup trucks and four cars in the parking lot looked as if they belonged to the English but she saw no signs of Amish life.

Maybe Levi lived within walking distance.

Kay reversed her car and pulled onto the road.

Strange feelings of isolation and longing mixed together inside her. The earth smell of sulfur from the coal mines mixed with the aroma of rich black soil and fresh wildflowers that called to her.

No other place smelled like the Holmes County of her childhood... at least no other place that she'd visited.

But...

She still felt the weight of her dress from childhood. Each mile she drove seemed to press its imaginary front panel tighter on her chest.

"When Eve sinned she tempted Adam," Bishop Benjamin had preached. "Therefore women must cover their bodies and be subject to men."

Kay shuddered.

Before she left this place her dark clothing protected her from the lusts of men... and trapped the summer heat inside her skin.

How did her sisters stand it?

The air caught in Kay's throat.

Maybe she shouldn't have come.

Two Amish women drove their buggy up the side of the road and stopped to wait for traffic. A group of children stood in the compartment behind their seat. If Kay had just passed her sisters she wouldn't even recognize them.

No wonder the Amish avoided people like her.

How could they make their members obey the Ordnung, or the Old German rules for living, when one of their own tempted them away?

Her nieces and nephews would stare at her worldly English clothing and fancy car.

Unaware of her attempted modesty.

Frightened by her wicked behavior.

They'd wonder how she escaped the wrath of Got.

Build That Wall

<< ☼ >>

 The electric lines stopped at the corner of Spooky Hollow Road just as they had done the day Kay left home. At least one thing stayed the same.
 Steel carriage rims burnt deeper into the macadam.
 Horseshoes made a sharper ridge.
 Little else looked different
 The smell of fresh manure drifted across the field of her parent's farm.
 A man walked behind two Clydesdales – the clack, thump, rattle of a spreader reminded Kay of why she'd felt so connected to this place.
 A line of geese waddled through the front yard to a small ditch. They lowered their beaks in the stream... then raised their heads to let water flow down their long necks.
 "Honk. Honk." Kay heard their noisy clatter.
 Mother never had any use for those dirty birds but now they waddled back and forth on her parents' farm.
 Kay remembered watching new hatchlings struggle to fit themselves back into their broken shelters. Expecting this land to contain her would be as useless as forcing a gosling back inside its shell.
 She turned in at her parents' driveway.
 The click clack... click click clack of the windmill sounded its job of pumping water into the animal trough.
 Autumn's dog ran to the car and barked his welcome.
 "Come on Merlin." Little Joe walked around the corner of the white frame house and grabbed the animal's collar.
 No. Not Little Joe.
 Must be little Joe's son – close to the age Joey had been 16 years earlier.
 "Aach. Come on now." Mother came through the door of the summer kitchen toward the car and wiped her hands on her apron.

"It's chust so wonderful nice to see you. Levi should be here any time now."

Kay remembered that day twenty six years earlier when she cut up apples with her butter knife for the sauce they made in that very same summer kitchen.

A child toddled through the steam and held out her hand.

"Do you want some, Charity?" Kay had said.

Whap!

Kay landed on the floor from the force of Mam's flying wooden spoon.

"There will be no witchcraft in this house." Mam spoke in her quiet, no nonsense voice.

Later that day Kay talked to her cousin Autumn. "You have a gift. You just saw back to the time when your sister still lived. In the Old Testament they called people like you seers. Just don't tell your Mam what you see and you can't get in trouble."

From that day on Kay had changed her thinking. She always thought of her mam in the more formal, and safer, English name of Mother.

She decided to leave this way of life as soon as she could. For sure and certain!

Maybe Kay made a mistake coming back here.

But Autumn's stepson, Harley, had insisted.

Kay opened her car door and hoped her face betrayed none of the emotions that swirled through her body.

Chapter 2

"It's been awhile." Kay left her car and walked to Mother to shake her hand. A chill ran up through her arm.

The Ordnung defines the life of my family of origin... Kay reminded herself. But after all this time she'd thought it could be different... that they could leave the hurt in the past.

"Your flowers came out nice this year." Kay looked at the rows of day lilies. Purple and lavender. White. Orange and yellow. New blooms framed the house.

"Jah. Been experimenting we have. Trying our hand at Grandma B's herbal remedies too." Relief shown on her mother's face. "Good you could come. Priscilla and Hope should be on their way now yet."

Mother turned to Little Joe. "Go get your daudi," she said.

"Are you Tanta Katie? Annie and Andy's mam?" The little boy stood with his hands on the white Pyrenees' collar.

"Yes." Kay knelt down to his level and petted the dog. "I suppose that you're my Brother Joey's boy. How do you come to have Merlin?"

"Cousin Harley left him with me for a few days. Merlin likes me," he said.

"You look just like your father," Kay said.

The boy nodded. His knowing brown eyes – Troyer eyes – shown from under an Amish straw hat.

His long sleeved blue homemade shirt... Suspenders to keep his black pants from falling off his skinny little body... His red bowl-cut hair replicated the Joey Kay had left behind.

Innocent.

Yet older than his age.

She grabbed him and hugged him to her. "I've missed you so much."

"Tanta Katie." The little boy wiggled out of her grasp.

"You're right." Kay released him. Stood and watched him scurry off to talk to his dad.

She imagined how red his face must be.

Her Amish family didn't give in to such shows of emotion.

"Any time now then. Driving over your sisters Priscilla and Hope should be." Mother repeated herself. Maybe she felt nervous too.

"Where's Harley with my children?" Kay tried to see the farm through her twins' eyes.

Horses.

Good food.

Baths once a week.

No need for shoes.

Of course they loved this place.

No worries about the Ordnung for them.

"At Aunt Sadie's yet. Fixing up the bed and breakfast Harley's been. Goodness sakes. Until he drove up to her door Sadie didn't even know she had a grandson." Mother's voice held the same tone of reproach Kay remembered from her childhood.

Autumn should have told Aunt Sadie about Harley.

And Kay hadn't written home since she left sixteen years ago.

Oh well.

"I guess Harley and Aunt Sadie are getting along." Kay said.

"Of course they are," Mother said. "Why wouldn't they?"

Her question was more of a statement of fact. She didn't expect a response.

"Levi's been over there too," Mother said. "He helped Harley replace the front porch and then he gave Aunt Sadie four rockers for her guests and then two more for your children."

Now Mother's tone of voice seemed to point condemnation toward Kay... as if Mother knew Kay had turned down Levi's proposal of marriage... as if Kay SHOULD have been grateful for the affections of a man who was better than she deserved... as if Kay SHOULD FINALLY do the right thing.

Whatever that was.

Build That Wall

Kay watched Little Joe talk to the man who drove the team of horses.

He nodded. Then started again.

Manure flew out from the back of the wagon behind him.

Kay hadn't been bothered by the strong smell of a barn-cleaning. She must be more nervous than she'd thought.

She recognized signs of the whole family planning to gather... the women would come first to set out the food and the men would stop their work before dark.

It wasn't even a Sunday.

Kay tried to remember the last time that happened.

Her cousin's wedding... in November after the crops were in... not in the middle of the summer when work needed doing.

Maybe a few times a year they'd have a gathering on a Saturday night in the summer before a preaching Sunday.

This must be one of those times.

Did they actually believe they might bring her back to the Amish community? They'd NEVER accept her divorce.

"Lemonade and iced tea I made. Come into the kitchen, why don't you?" Mother hustled to the door of the big house without waiting for Kay's answer... then turned toward the road.

"Well look who it is," she said. "There's a nice breeze out. Sit on the porch. Why don't you?"

She hurried inside and left Kay on the sidewalk.

A black Sting Ray inched up the driveway next to the gaggle of geese. The classic car appeared to be a twin to the silver one Kay had sold in Quakertown Pennsylvania.

It made sense.

Levi who had owned the friskiest horse in Amish country now drove a high performance car.

It seemed as if he could afford it.

How did he manage to pick the same model she drove?

The same year even...

He left the Amish.

The Amish Time Traveler

That was for sure and certain.

When Kay left this place she thought she'd changed her choices. Changed everything about herself.

Had she?

On what unconscious level were Levi and she enough alike to drive the same year of a Corvette?

He parked behind her rental car and stepped on the driveway.

Balding brown hair.

Built like a middle aged weight lifter...

Levi reminded her of the young Amish man she'd left behind her but his checkered button down shirt and khaki slacks covered the sculpted body of a meticulous middle class man who had survived some of life's potholes and found a certain rhythm.

"Hi Katie." He spoke as if they'd seen each other yesterday.

She felt her body respond with comfortable recognition. In what parallel universe had her life in Holmes County stopped and waited for her return?

Kay stared at him... unable to speak.

How could she show up at a family reunion after sixteen years and feel as if she hadn't left?

Why had she moved to another state and changed her whole life when it seemed to make so little difference?

Kay peered at his feet. Her cordovan loafers looked as if they'd been made by the same manufacturer as his.

What happened to her creative edge... her seemingly unorthodox choices?

How had they both shown up with the same color button down shirts... and the same shoes? How had she worn a skirt fabric to match his pants?

How unoriginal.

Kay lifted her hands to her face and touched her skin.

Did they look alike?

The Path not Taken. Was it Robert Frost? Kay couldn't remember. Levi was her path not taken. What if she'd stayed here? What if...

Build That Wall

Kay's legs felt wooden but somehow she led Levi to the porch and walked to the far rocker.

Had Levi made these chairs too? She wondered.

"I brought some tea and cookies." Mother set the plain tray on a small table. "Supper should be ready in about an hour. Are you hungry?"

"Thank you Mrs. Troyer." Levi hopped up and helped Mother pour two glasses of tea... then sat next to Kay in his matching seat.

Kay stared into the field across the road unable to speak.

"I met your children – they remind me of you when you were little," Levi said.

"Thanks. I'm not home enough though," Kay said. Her mother had stayed on the farm all day every day.

Kay lifted the glass to her mouth and dribbled tea down the front of her shirt. Why was she so nervous? It was only Levi.

"They look well-loved," Levi said. "I can't imagine they could have had a better mother."

He moved back and forth in the chair as if to ease the tension for them both. He appeared smaller than he had sixteen years earlier. Less imposing. A bit defenseless.

"Thank you. I do my best," Kay said. Did he know she filed for divorce?

Why else would he be talking like this? But even if he had joined the Mennonites – they didn't like divorce either.

Or did they by now?

Maybe his congregation accepted it.

"Andy claims he's surprised how his mom had such a great life. He didn't know about it until he came here with Harley. He said you only talk about the grandma in the cemetery," Levi said. "Then Annie told us about Autumn's husband. Is he really in an urn on the shelf so he can watch her?"

"Autumn doesn't hold to the Amish custom where women keep silent and revere their men no matter what," Kay said. "He kept telling her she'd never survive without him. Now she says he has to watch. I bet that caused a stir around here."

The Amish Time Traveler

"She always was one of a kind. That cousin of yours." Levi shook his head and laughed. "The folks around her will repeat her stories for years... but I'm glad you have her. I've prayed for you every day since you left. Except when I was married, that is."

Goosebumps ran across Kay's arms... up and down her spine.

This man had been devoted.

Honest.

Good.

And now successful.

"Mother said your wife died," Kay said. "I'm sorry to hear it."

"She was widowed and a couple of years older. I helped raise her children. They're grown now. We didn't have any of our own." The pain of his words found their target.

The center of Kay's heart.

"They say that life's what happens when you've made other plans," she said.

"I always wonder who they are." Levi laughed. "Complete strangers. Or are they the same people we call everybody when we want to shift the rules?"

"Makes you think," Kay said.

What would he say about her travels to 18th century England and 16th century Europe?

Would he still pray for her if he knew?

Or would he try to save her soul from hell?

He'd probably approve of her visit to the time of Menno Simons – the founder of the Mennonites and Amish.

Chapter 3

Harley's four wheel drive truck shifted down and turned in the lane.

"Looks your twins are here," Levi said.

Kay left him on the porch and ran to the driveway. Threw open the passenger door and grabbed her children. "I've missed you so much."

"Mom, you're squishing me." Andrew wriggled away from her. "I hope you weren't worried about us when you went to England 'cause we're o.k. Harley took us to a rodeo last night. He said it's not a real rodeo like they have in the West but it had lots of animals. When I grow up Uncle Joe said I can come back here and be Amish if I want to. Did you see the new puppies? I've got to go see Merlina. "

"Not yet," Kay said. "I..."

Annie interrupted her. "We've got lots and lots of cousins. We even stayed here on the farm one night and Uncle Joseph said I slept in your old room. They have horses and we rode in their carriage and picked some peas. Grandma Troyer said it was the last batch until fall and we ate them right out in the garden and they have a work horse named Jack." Annie took a breath. "We got to brush him when Uncle Joseph brought him in from raking the hay. They put it in piles so the animals can eat it in the winter and I helped Grandma Troyer can some peas in the summer kitchen because they have two kitchens. One for the winter and one for the summer when it's too hot to cook inside. And Grandma said Andy can stay the rest of the summer and I want to help out with Great-aunt Sadie. She pays me a fifty cents an hour. When Aunt Hope and Aunt Priscilla get here you can meet our cousins Anne and Andrew. Did you meet Jack? We got to brush him when Uncle Joseph brought him in from raking the hay. Do you want t' go find him?"

"Jack must be your Uncle Joey's horse," Kay said. "I'll...

"Come on Annie. Let's go find the puppies," Andrew came back to grab her hand and pull her to the barn.

"Love you." Kay swallowed a lump of jealousy.

The twins should have missed her more than this.

"Hi Cuz." Harley's came around the truck and gave her a hug. "You want me to march them back here and instruct them to give you a somber rendition of how much they miss you?"

"Just don't tell me it's part of your 12 step program to steal my kids," Kay said.

"They did talk about you while you were off traveling with my mom. They can't believe you lived this exciting life and didn't tell them about it. Andy wants to use a lantern and wood stove all of the time. He said he's going to be Amish when he grows up. He talked your brother Joseph into letting him stay for the rest of the summer if it's O.K. with you."

Kay's chest restricted. If Andrew moved back to Holmes County she could be ostracized from her mother and from her son.

"You're quiet. Did I say something wrong?" Harley said.

"Is Andrew serious?" Did Kay's own mother feel this way when Kay left home?

"He's a kid. He'll have lots of other ideas before he grows up," Harley said.

"I knew what I wanted when I was six years old." And no one could change Kay's mind.

"By the way, your mom seems happy to have you here. She said that since you never joined the church you'll be treated like any other English relative," Harley said.

"Did you mention the divorce?" Kay said.

"No but the twins told her they have a new house. Their dad lives in the old house."

"What did she say about that?"

"Nothing. But when we were alone she said it took a lot of courage to go off on your own like you did."

Right. And that's all she'd say.

The Amish weren't called the quiet in the land for nothing. Her mother ignored unpleasantries.

"She may want to see me but I'm sure she won't begin to listen to anything about my fancy English trip," Kay said. Mother would pretend to be deaf if Kay mentioned time travel or any other fancy nonsense.

"You and my mom must have felt like you were in jail when you lived here. By the way, I talked to her on the phone. She said went to a place called Eden Manor near Oxford University and that you found an amulet to take you back to the time of Queen Anne." he said.

"I've never seen Autumn so excited. But the real question is: how did you get my mother to buy me a ticket from JFK to the New Philadelphia Airport? She believes that Satan's the prince of the air, you know." Kay let out a sigh.

How did her family live by such ridiculous rules?

"Well," Harley said. "She didn't actually buy the ticket. She gave me the money and said I could keep the change as long as I got you here. She didn't actually say you should fly but I think she knew what would happen."

"Right," Kay said. "I knew you were taking a road trip when I left for England, but I thought you'd have them home by now. When I found out you were here I felt as if I had to come... as if you didn't give me a choice."

"You can yell at me later. Right now I'm worried about her. She gave me cash in small bills... as if she saved for a long time and hid it from your father. I felt guilty taking it. Should we pay her back?"

"No!" Kay said. "She'd be offended. NOTHING is more important to her than her family. Now, whether I stay five minutes of five months, she'll be able to say that all of her children came to see her at once and she'll know that she helped make it possible."

"But she gave me too much money," Harley said.

"It's a matter of pride," Kay said. "Whatever you do, don't try to pay her back. She'll be offended. Andrew's coming back, we'll talk about it later..."

The Amish Time Traveler

"Mom." Andrew led a White Pyrenees puppy up to them. "This is Merlina. She's the best bitch in the world."

Kay wondered about her family. When she lived here they had laughed at the stupid city slickers who thought potatoes grew on trees and bulls gave milk. What stories did they tell about her twins? Did it matter? Or did Uncle Joseph, as the twins called him, forbid them to make fun of Annie and Andrew?

"Aunt Priscilla and Aunt Hope are here!" Annie ran from the barn and stood in the driveway waiting for the buggy that turned toward the house.

Kay followed the twins' eyes to see the carriage she'd passed on Route 39 — the one driven by two women with a group of children standing in front of the back seat.

She hadn't recognized her own family.

"Is that why you changed your name to Andy?" Kay said. "So people won't confuse you with your cousin, Andrew?"

Her boy nodded as if his mind were on the carriage and he'd forgotten everything else.

Kay stood behind the twins and laid her hands on their shoulders until her sisters stopped the horse.

"Can we take something in?" Annie and Andy ran to their aunts and spoke in unison.

Merlina barked her welcome to the other children.

Levi came from the lawn where he'd been helping Mother set up tables and stood by the horse. "Should I tie your horse to the post or take her to the barn?" he said.

Kay had forgotten how the Amish don't wait to help each other.

They see work as a communal effort.

Kay felt as if she were the prodigal daughter.

Her nieces and nephews stared at her as if they were frightened by her worldly English clothes and wondered how she escaped the wrath of Got.

So much for her attempt at modesty.

"You have a sister you haven't even met," Andy said.

A midget climbed down from the buggy.

"Aunt Charity. This is my mom," Annie said. "Mom. This is your sister. Aunt Charity."

"Hi Katie." The girl grabbed Kay's waist. "Joey told me all about you."

Charity released her and ran to fling her arms around Mother in a hug. "I missed you sooo much!"

"You've only been gone for three days." Mother spoke with a softness Kay had never heard from her before.

Charity stood back from Mother with her feet apart and her hands on her hips.

"When we were in the store I heard some English girls talking about sex," she said. "I asked Hope to tell me what sex is but she said I have to ask you."

"Humph." Mother let out her breath in a sigh as if she hated to speak of such things.

She stood a bit straighter and faced Charity.

"Well, she said. "I'm sure you've seen a bull jump on the back of a cow and put his penis inside her. Haven't you?"

"Sure," Charity said. "That's how they get calves."

"That's called sex," Mother said. "If..."

Charity interrupted her.

"I have to go to the pasture and check on the cows." She ran to the barn as if she'd forgotten everyone around her.

"See what you missed," Hope said.

"Wow." Kay stared after her little sister. "How old is she?"

"Fourteen. Same as a six year old," Priscilla said.

"I like her. She replaced the Charity who died, I guess," Kay said.

Hope shrugged. "You could say that."

Kay felt as if her family formed a blanket of protection around this special girl... as if they relaxed the strict Ordnung to give Charity more freedoms than they'd extent to a normal child.

Mother seemed relieved to have given give birth to another daughter she understood rather than the Kay who'd seemed English even from her childhood.

"Now. Home. All four of my daughters came – and Elizabeth by dark will be here chust like it should be." Mother's face beamed with joy. "And all of my grandchildren I know."

"Who's Elizabeth?" Kay said.

"Soon enough you'll meet," Mother said.

Kay's family had seemed to gather for her return. She was still these people's sister, daughter, aunt, niece, and almost ex-fiancé. The bishop approved of this visit but why was Mother this excited?

Priscilla and Hope would probably talk about their children and give her some recipes she'd never use. Then they'd ask her some embarrassing questions to point out how English she'd become.

Still....

"You look good in the face even if you did leave us. To England I heard you went," Hope said. "How did it feel to see your own country?"

Kay felt the edge to Hope's voice.

Jealousy?

Condemnation?

Kay never felt as if she quite understood Hope's disapproval of her. Maybe Hope didn't even know it herself.

"Sorry but I'll have to say the hellos after I get the food inside." Priscilla handed an infant to her adolescent daughter, then held her wicker picnic basket in both hands.

"Let me help you," Kay said. "Can I take something in?"

"No. Everything's covered." Hope retrieved her baby from the carriage.

"My Annie. Two weeks old. Her first time out." Hope shifted the child in her arms and moved the light blanket from her daughter's face.

"Nice to meet you." Kay touched Annie's soft cheek and felt a surge of love replace any irritation she'd felt toward her family. "Can I hold her?"

"Sure." Hope handed the baby over and Kay felt her organic kinship with this small bundle.

In that instance it seemed as if this communal socialism seeped into Kay's bones. She became one with the Amish connection where every adult cared for each other's children as if they were their own.

Unlike their English neighbors the Amish left none of their members to rely on social welfare.

Her sisters talked to her as if she were the same clumsy girl who would never learn but at that moment Kay didn't mind. Baby Annie felt as close to her as if she were Kay's own newborn daughter.

The child started to cry and Kay held her out to her mother.

"Don't forget." Hope opened a small seam in the front of her dress and held the baby to her nipple. "You'll always be MY LITTLE SISTER."

"Of course," Kay said. "And you'll ALWAYS be my big sister."

If anything bad ever happened to Hope, Kay would raise baby Annie without question – even though no one would ask it of an English outsider. And if anything ever happened to Kay or her children Hope would make certain their needs were met even if they didn't ask.

Chapter 4

Kay looked for her own children but it seemed as if they'd run off to play with their cousins.

Kay reverted to her childhood habit of wandering around the side of the house to the ancient porch swing. It still hung by the lilac bushes where she remembered it back when life made no sense at all and she'd considered joining the Amish to marry the most eligible bachelor in Holmes County.

"I remember you here." Levi walked toward her. "Your sisters used to treat you like a dumb-Kopf back then too."

"The first time I've left my children for more than a night or two and they hardly notice when get I get back."

"Independence is a good thing. Your children know you're there for them. No matter what. Otherwise they'd be afraid to stay here without you." Levi slipped onto the seat next to her.

Resumed the back and forth rhythm.

The faint rotten egg smell from the strip mines mixed with the odor of a fresh cleaned barn wafted an uncertain peace across the country air.

"I'm trying to imagine telling some of my city slicker friends how the smell of sulfur and fresh cow manure feels reassuring." Kay wouldn't mention how Philadelphia Main Liners saw her home in Quakertown as "the hicks."

Compared to this place Quakertown seemed urbane.

"They say you can't take the country out of the girl." Levi spoke as if he hoped his words contained some truth. "I don't think you can take the Amish out either."

"I've been gone for a bit more than half of my life. Things look different after that," Kay said.

"Andy told her you moved and you guys don't see him anymore."

The swing slowed.

His body seemed to grow rigid as if his world revolved around Kay's answer.

"I bought the house next to Autumn and signed the farm over to my ex. The divorce should be final." The facts. Plain and simple. Like her Amish childhood.

"You took my sunshine when you left. If I'd given you more time." He paused as if he were uncertain how to finish the sentence.

"I can't answer that," she said

"Is there someone else now?" Levi grew up Amish. He may have left the church but his whole countenance reminded Kay how he valued the truth.

She refused to fudge it now.

"I just left my husband a couple of months ago. Then I encountered a friend from the past named Steve but he's gone too. I'm not ready for any decisions. Not now," she said.

"I'd be happy to build you a house here or in Quakertown. I don't have permanent ties anywhere except for relatives I could visit from a distance," Levi said. "I always felt that God wants us together."

"You're certainty frightens me." Kay wondered if she should tell him that she possessed an amulet of Zipporah to help her see through time just like Samuel and the prophets of the Old Testament who were called Seers.

Could he accept that in a wife?

"I lived in my ex-husband's house. His mom wanted it to be in my name but he always acted as if it was his and his alone. I need to make my own way this time," Kay said.

"I agree with you. When you turned sixteen I felt different but then I saw how my wife's first husband left her destitute with two children. I wouldn't ever want that for you. But I lost you once and I don't want it to happen again," Levi said.

Kay read the truth in his eyes.

The Amish Time Traveler

The Levi she'd left behind had been so sure he had all of the answers. The man today seemed confident but ready to learn.

"I'm sorry I didn't write," Kay said. "I meant to but I was afraid you'd hope too much. Then I met my husband."

Kay remembered how proud she felt when he promised to buy her a diamond. How much she'd wanted to show off her pretty ring and watch the look on her mother's face.

"Things didn't work out the way I thought," Kay said. "Conrad will never be the man you are but he seemed so exciting to a naïve country girl like me. I felt as if I couldn't help myself around him. Now I just feel used."

An awkward silence cut the air between them.

Levi pushed their swing back and forth in a slow rhythm. They watched Merlin scamper toward the geese barking and wagging his tail.

A half dozen goslings tried to fly.

Then floundered.

The gaggle ran at Merlin. Honking. Nipping his ears.

He yelped and ran.

Tail between his legs.

"That looked like it hurt," Levi said.

Merlin headed toward the porch where Joey stood.

"Silly boy." Joey patted the dog's head. "Veste sie. Learn. You never will. Never let you get their babies those mams will."

Merlin sat in front of him and wagged his tail as if he'd just returned from a grand adventure. His tongue rolled off the side of his mouth.

"He's laughing. Looks like." Levi scratched his head. "He likes the game."

"Yah," Kay said. "The thrill of the chase."

"Isn't it a nice evening?" he said.

"Yah but two of the geese look like they can't keep up with the others," Kay said. "What's with that?"

"It's Charity's doing," Levi said. "A blind drake wandered into the farm and Charity fell in love with him. She got your mam to put

Build That Wall

an ad in the paper but no one claimed him so a neighbor brought a girlfriend for company and there you have it. A seeing-eye goose and her family."

"Do you mean all the other geese are her children?" Kay said.

"Yip. And I bet those two fowl will never find the cooking pot," Levi said.

Kay listened to the quiet clacking of the windmill and settled into the comfort of silence that she and Levi seemed to enjoy.

She tried to imagine her mother adopting a lame goose when Kay was a child. The image refused to compute.

A gentle breeze floated toward them. Cooler and less humid than it'd be in a month or so.

She removed her shoes and felt the earth's energy rise up through her feet. Nurture her. Give her peace.

"Wonderbar gutte." She borrowed a Pennsylvania Dutch saying. Wonderful good.

She remembered the last time she'd sat here with Levi.

Chapter 5

Sixteen years earlier Levi had led her to his courting buggy. Unhitched Black Lightening and flicked the reins.

The clack clickity clack of the horse and carriage had accompanied Kay's quiet screams.

Some book described the Amish as the quiet in the land but they failed to describe the deafening roar of unspoken pain – how an Amish man's two well-placed words could initiate a tidal wave of despair.

But after riding a couple miles Kay had grasped these last moments to her. She'd found a bit of peace in the natural conversations of the earth. The blurb of the bullfrog.

The song of crickets. The hoot of an owl.

That same quiet space might turn rancid in a moment. Trap a simmering cauldron of hidden pain.

Kay shook the thought from her head.

<< ☼ >>

"The anonymous they say that you're as sick as your secrets." Levi's voice brought Kay back to the present time.

He stared at the lilac bush in front of them. Ruffled white daylilies rimmed its trunk.

Kay wondered if he'd read her mind.

"I've unloaded most of my private skeletons on poor Autumn." Kay bent and picked one daylily – so-called because it blooms for one day.

"I planned to join the church after you left but I couldn't do it," Levi said. "I rented my properties and went to Eastern Mennonite College hoping you'd catch up to me there. When I heard you married I signed up with MCC." [1]

---

[1] Mennonite Central Committee, a mission agency designed to help relieve poverty through spiritual enrichment, micro business management and community aide.

"I had no idea," Kay said. Maybe they could have gone to college together. Maybe she hadn't needed to leave here.

"At least you were honest. You didn't lead me on," Levi said. "I got to spend two years in Nepal helping a poor village dig a well. Helping them farm. Next to them the Amish live a very modern life. Then I married my best friend and helped her raise her two children."

"I'm not used to such loyalty," Kay said.

"I'm not your family. They love you in their own way, but they don't see you the way I do."

"So you're Mennonite now?"

"I joined the Mennonites a couple of years after you left. My wife was Mennonite. Her children are grown now. Rebecca's Methodist and Ben's Baptist," Levi said.

Was he saying that he'd attend any church with her?

Some Amish believed that God provided only one person for the perfect partner but Kay had never heard of a man who changed his religion for his wife.

All Amish men felt obligated to rule their own homes.

"I'm not like I was before," Levi said.

Had he read her mind again?

"Nepal changed me. If we preach that God loves everyone why do we need the Ordnung?" he said.

What happened to the Levi who'd planned Kay's life within its certain mold?

"I'm not even like I was last year. My wife's death showed me how little time we have."

"My mother in law's death changed my life," Kay said. "I think I liked her more than I liked her son."

"My wife taught me not to make decisions for other people. That's what I did with you. I didn't even ask what you wanted," Levi said.

"I'm sure you made a wonderful husband." Not exciting like Conrad or Sven... but good. And kind.

"There you two are." Mother's voice came from the behind them. "Get yourselves to the table for supper onct' and eat yourselves full."

She sounded way too pleased to find them here. Alone.

Did she want Kay to move back to Holmes County and marry Levi?

Neither of them were Amish.

Had Kay missed a chapter in or Mother's own private book of rules?

Chapter 6

Kay hadn't eaten home-made food like this since she'd left here after her sixteenth birthday.

The celebratory seven sours came from a tradition of limited refrigeration. Chow chow, three bean salad, end of the garden pickles, green tomato pickles, bread and butter pickles, pickled red beets, and pickled hard boiled eggs.

And Mother's seven sweets came from the pump house and the pie cupboard. German chocolate cake, funny cake, ground cherry pie, tapioca, graham cracker pudding, whoopee pies and oatmeal coconut cookies. Her sisters added chocolate sauerkraut cake with peanut butter cream cheese frosting and pumpkin ganache pie.

Platters of ham, chicken and roast beef decorated the table along with sweet potatoes, scalloped potatoes, and three kinds of potato salad, Jell-O, fresh breads and rolls.

Amish farmers worked hard and ate high-fat sugary food.

A gulf of hunger opened within Kay filled with memories of the real food Mother started from seeds and nurtured with years of manure and compost.

On non-preaching Sundays when her family visited relatives Kay and her friends stuffed themselves with their noon-time dinners until they could hardly walk.

Tonight the men laid planks on saw horses and the women covered them with tablecloths.

Kay's brothers and sisters had seemed to appear as if by magic with a flock of children dressed in identical clothing.

They all stood waiting in the silent prayer.

"Amen," Father said.

Chatter started as if on cue.

Talk about the crops.

The new bishop.

Weather.

Charity sided up to Kay. "Do you know the definition of an Amish man?" she said.

"No but you can tell me."

"Someone who can buy from a Scotsman. Sell to a Jew. And make a profit." Charity looked up at Kay to gauge her reaction.

"That sure is," Kay said. She patted Charity on the back.

"Are you behaving yourself Charity?" Mother came up to them as if she were checking to make sure her youngest daughter didn't say anything to embarrass Kay.

"We're good," Kay said.

"Don't forget to eat your vegetables now Charity," Mother said.

"Where'd you hear that joke?" Levi said.

"I don't know. I just heard it." Charity stepped up to the table with whoopee pies and swiped several to hide behind her apron.

If Kay hadn't seen it she wouldn't have believed it. She caught Charity's eye and winked.

"Do you know any Scotsmen or Jews?" Levi said.

"No. But I seen a Scottie. It's a dog," Charity said.

"You're a real good joke teller Charity." Kay winked again and Charity disappeared around the corner of the house.

Several people around them laughed. Then passed the joke on to others. It seemed politically incorrect with a grain of truth. Kay reasoned. Her Amish family hoarded their few pennies more than anyone else she knew.

She watched the men shovel food on their plates.

Men over the age of sixteen always ate first because they had just come in from the fields.

Mothers helped their children next and then ate last.

"How do they even know about Jews and Scotts?" Kay said. "I thought everyone non-Amish seemed the same."

"Things change. At least a few things." Levi stayed back and served himself with the women. "Land is getting harder and harder to buy. I employ some of my relatives in my shop and half of them have to bargain with the English six days a week."

Still....

Build That Wall

An invisible umbilical cord tied her to these plain folk as if an earthen rope knotted her to their genetic makeup.

Her own children seemed to feel the same kinship as if the uniform dress of their cousins gave them a comfortable sense of social unity.

Even though Annie and Andy asked more questions than all of their quiet cousins combined nobody seemed to object to them.

"Andy's planning to join the Amish." Levi cleared his throat to suppress a smile. "Your nieces and nephews haven't even played one trick on either of them. Not even one snipe hunt."

"That's amazing," Kay said. "How'd they manage that?"

"Your children are charming. And they're smart. They know enough about farm work and animals that they fit right in," he said.

"When I was a kid one of Mother's fancy English friends went to the hospital and left her mentally challenged son with us," Kay said.

"She'd never met your brother Matthias." Levi looked into Kay's eyes as if to say that he knew how Matt had treated her.

A slice of secret pain slid off Kay's shoulders.

"Thanks." Kay sighed. She felt overwhelmed by the unusual understanding of this man who'd shared the same childhood.

"We all played the *snipe hunting trick* on each other. For us Amish kids it was a big joke to give the new kid a bag and tell him to wait in the field while we chased snipes to him," he said.

"Wow," Kay said. "We were little con artists weren't we? We convinced our own 13 year old cousins they could get a full-grown wild bird into a pillowcase without a fight."

Levi shook his head as if in wonder.

"I think it was the power of the crowd. When we asked a younger boy to prove he's not a coward he'd do anything to show us we were wrong," he said. "I never thought of ourselves as conning them but you're right. We were manipulative little brats."

"We weren't supposed to fight but sometimes we made up for it with passive aggression," Kay said.

"But your brother Matt was something else. He gave the nervous English kid a pillow case and took him out to the field right before dark," Levi said. "Matt threatened the kid with bodily harm if he moved, then left."

"We knew how to take care of ourselves but the English kid would still be out there if Mother hadn't noticed he was gone. I saw him a few years later and he ran from me as if he were still scared."

"Did Matt get in trouble?" Levi said.

"Never heard of it if he did. You know how my mother treats her menfolk," Kay said. "He left for rumspringa[2] soon after."

"The English kid got away from him but you lived in fear. I always hated that," Levi said

"Ja. Youngest daughter and all that. We don't fare too well in this family," Kay said

"Especially when the men are always right and they seem to be afraid of the women's ideas," Levi said.

"Mom." Annie ran up to them and tugged on Kay's arm. "Is Andy another name for God?"

"No where'd you get that idea?" Kay said

"Andy walks with me Andy talks with me. Like in the song. Andy said he's just like God," Annie said.

Kay tensed the muscles in her mouth so she wouldn't laugh. "It's not Andy they're singing about. The words are AND HE. And. He. Walks with me."

Annie ran away. "Told you so Andy! It's AND... HE! Mom said."

"I love your kids." Levi laughed. "They're just like you. Saying the funniest things. I'm glad you don't punish them for speaking their minds. I think you may have been right to leave us back then. Give us a new perspective."

---

[2] Rumspringa, translated as the running round years, is that period of time after Amish children reach the age of 16 and before they are baptized into the church. During this time many bishops allow their young people to experience the freedoms of the English world before they submit to the authority of the church.

Chapter 7

"There you are, Katie. Glad to have you back." Father extended his hand and shook hers.

Waves of disgust traveled up through Kay's shoulder... and turned the sky to sulfur gray.

Had Father misunderstood?

Did he think she came back here to live?

"Good to see you son." Father shook Levi's hand with even more gusto.

Of course.

In Father's mind even a dumb-Kopf or stupid person like his little Katie knew enough to say yes to the most eligible widower in Holmes County?

"I have to check on my children." Kay ran to the corner of the house.

What was wrong with her?

An adult educated woman with her own business and one handshake from the male sperm donor sent her running.

Male sperm donor?

She'd rebelled against the patriarchal Ordnung or Amish rules for living since she could remember. But the anger. The pain of Father's presence surprised her.

Kay rushed to the outhouse and locked herself inside. She'd come here to make peace with her past, not to create a scene.

At Eden Manor she'd understood why she'd been born Amish. But now....

Why did disquiet creep through her body"?

Father insisted on living his religion. He fed his animals before he ate his own meals.

His words defined him. He bound himself to each one even paying an English fine before speaking a falsehood.

He forbade the swearing of an oath and Kay had never heard him curse.

On the other hand keeping secrets. That seemed normal.

Had Kay hidden her own childhood memories? She shook the thought from her head. The Amish countryside seemed to play tricks with her mind.

<< ☼ >>

Someone pushed on the outhouse door.

"Just a minute." Kay stepped out.

"It's you." Her sister Priscilla held a hand of each of her own twins. "Levi looks friendly. Is there something we should know?"

Kay bent down to the girls. "And what are your names?"

Each of Kay's nieces peeked an eye from behind their mother's skirt as if they feared their scary English aunt.

"This is Aunt Katie." Priscilla pulled her daughters forward. "Katie. My daughters. Ruth and Esther."

Kay took turns acknowledging them by the nod of her head.

"How can you be our aunt? You're English." Strands of Esther's strawberry curls stole from the edges of her kapp.

"Don't be rude." Priscilla pulled the girls into the outhouse as if Kay's touch were contagious.

It seemed clear that this reunion wasn't Priscilla's idea.

Kay wanted to take her own twins and leave this place.

Now.

"Did you see Priscilla? I thought I saw her come this way?" Kay's sister Hope stood on the sidewalk in front of her.

"In the outhouse with her twins," Kay said.

"Oh good." Hope rushed past her. Then hurried back to Kay as if she'd just remembered something. "You and Levi seem pretty cozy. What's up with you two?"

"I almost married him before I left," Kay said.

"You've gotta be kiddin' me." Hope jostled her child in her arms. Her attitude of scorn seemed to turn to silent respect.

"No kiddin'. Did Mother tell you that I found the name on my birth certificate? It's Kay English," Kay said.

"That s'posed to mean something?"

"Just confirmed what I knew about myself. You know I never fit in here. I was always different."

"That you were." Hope wriggled her nose as if thinking very hard. "That you were. But to turn down Levi... I never thought even you would do somethin' like that."

"A part of me will always be Amish. I was born here. I'm glad you enjoy your life. But I can't live the way you do. I need "forbidden" books, cars and even airplanes but who am I to judge our differences? Menno Simons was a true revolutionary."

"An Anabaptist you mean," Hope said. "He was an Anabaptist."

"Ja. That too." Kay remembered her visit to the small village of 16th century Austria. Pauline's dying wish had been to meet the priest who preached a Christian socialist equality of peace modeled after the early church – a man who cut through the hierarchical systems of religion and treated all of his followers as if they were his own brothers and sisters.

The Ordnung or rules for living had seemed so much more sensible compared to Popish rules which kept them in dire poverty. Maybe Priscilla and Hope found their own brand of peace this way.

Chapter 8

The half-moon sneaked its translucent form toward the top of the sky.

Kay needed to play nice for a few more hours.

Help Mother feel complete.

She'd see the rest of her siblings.

Maybe some aunts and uncles.

Cousins.

Then she'd take her twins and go.

The bishop wouldn't want her to stay too long anyway lest her worldly English lifestyle pollute the minds of the kinder, the Amish children.

Kay would be gone before such a discussion.

She wandered over to the heaping tables full of food. She didn't feel hungry anymore but the familiar free-range fried chicken, German potato salad, pickled beets, homemade applesauce and fresh grown produce all called out to her.

"I have a joke." Charity sneaked up next to. "But don't tell Mam. She don't like it."

"You're such a blessing." Kay gave her baby sister a squeeze. "One we didn't even know we needed."

Charity wiggled out of Kay's grasp. She said:

> A man's car broke down in the middle of the road and he stood there waiting for help.
>
> A cow came up to him. "It's in the carburetor," the cow said.
>
> The English man jumped into his car and locked the doors.
>
> An Amish man stopped his buggy to help and the driver told his story.

"A big red cow with brown around one eye?" asked the Amish man.

"Yes, yes," the English man said.

"Don't go listenin' to Bessie," the Amish man said. "She don't know nothing 'bout cars."

Kay laughed and put her arm around Charity.

"You're a good joke teller Charity. And you make this family better just by being here," Kay said.

"Aww, now. Don't go makin' me proud." Charity lifted a whoopee pie from the dessert table.

"Mam went all out fer ja today," Charity said. "Don't tell nobody but I ate six already." She scooted around the corner of the house as if afraid someone might make her put it back.

"You go girl." Kay whispered after her.

"There you are. Those nasty skeeters. Eat us all... They will. On your arms rub some now. Then get you some more food. Eat." Mother held out a small mason jar filled with thick green liquid.

"What's in it?" Kay said.

"Lavender and vanilla in oil."

"Can you give me the recipe?" Kay tipped the quart canning jar and wet the small attached rag to pat some of the liquid on her exposed skin.

She'd make her own bug repellant at home for the twins.

"No trick to it," Mother said. "You just fill a jar with lavender and then pour oil over it and let it sit in the sun. Shake it up every day once for a week. Add a couple vanilla beans and there yah have it."

"Will do," Kay said.

"Gotta go," Mother said. "The men need more tea. You take this jar with you."

Chapter 9

Kay sneaked back to the swing with her supper. That familiar need to be alone settled over her. It seemed as if Mother liked the idea of having her here more than the fact of sitting and talking face to face. No one noticed her missing.

She finished the food on her plate... then nodded as if in a trance. A dream. A memory?

She looked down from above through a bright floating light of peace.

Earth. USA. Ohio. The Amish farm.

The woman stared at the ceiling. "NO!" she spoke in a quiet voice of desperation.

The man pushed himself into her. Then laid back exhausted. "Aah," he sighed and closed his eyes in contentment.

"No." Kay's spirit screamed. "No. No no no!"

"You've already agreed," her inner knowing demanded.

"I rescind! I didn't know it would be like this!" Kay's spirit resisted but her life-force slid down the blue light to earth and Ida Mae's alien womb.

The scene changed to Kay's last year of Amish school.

Eighth grade.

She walked home after class to twin lambs who butted the fence. "Baa. Baa," they called to her.

She took formula from the cupboard in the shed and measured equal amounts in each soda bottle. Then she added water from the hand pump and attached the nipples.

"Wiggles. Jiggles." She called to the orphaned babies. Their tiny black faces peeked from dirty white wool coats.

She opened the gate and lowered the nipples.

Build That Wall

They each grabbed one with their mouths and wiggled their whole bodies to push themselves against her as if she were their mother.

"Relax," Kay said. "Hurryin' makes waste."

They ignored her. Wagged their stubby tails as if in a race.

Their stomachs rounded while the bottles emptied. "That's enough. You're sucking air in your bellies." Kay laid the bottles down and sat on the thick grass beside them.

They tumbled over each other for a position on her lap.

"My babies." She rubbed her hands over their backs. Lanolin soaked her skin.

"Someday you'll grow up and give me your wool. Then you'll have babies and they'll give me theirs'. I'll sell it and follow Autumn East."

Their big brown eyes looked at her as if they were full of trust.

"Katie." Mother shouted across the fence. "There you are. Sitting on the ground with those dirty sheep crawling all over your school dress."

"Sorry Mother." Kay kissed each lamb on the forehead and laid them on the grass to sleep off their meals.

"It wonders me where you get your fancy English speakin'." Mother knelt in the garden to pick her peas. "Finish up quick and get the supper on onct'."

Her folks thought Kay raised sheep to save money for her wedding chest but she planned to move East with Autumn.

You were not ready to go to other dimensions, Kay's inner voice chided. You're just where you're supposed to be to learn your life lessons.

You still have work to do... other lives to visit so you find more acceptance of your journey. Look around at your family. Do they appear sad or without purpose? Who are you to say how they SHOULD live?

The Amish Time Traveler

Kay's family seemed to be smarter than most of her college professors. The English lost their farms in bankruptcy while the Amish bought more land.

Nature ordained their exact schedules. They rose before dawn and went to bed with the sun. Few of them left their way of life.

On the other hand her family called her dreamy and sought to keep her grounded. They taught her to think. To curb her desire to live by intuition alone.

They worked hard.

Prayed hard.

And thanked God for everything.

Now at 32 years old, Kay could enjoy being herself.

Returning to the Amish life seemed as impossible as hammering a square peg into a round hole. But no matter how far she traveled a part of that little Amish girl remained in her heart.

She would listen to that inner child. Value it.

Chapter 10

Kay headed back toward the tables.

"Hi Katie. We missed you." A young Amish man with a full red beard caught up to her.

"Little Joey? Is that you? All married and everything," Kay said.

Single men shaved their faces.

Husbands only shaved their mustaches.

"After you left it was never the same around here. But Annie and Andy are just like you. They make this place come alive. They told me you have a Sting Ray like Levi's!" Joey shook his head as if he were astounded Kay's English ways.

"I just sold it but that's not the most outrageous thing I've done. You'd never believe my life if I told you." Kay fake-punched her baby brother on the arm – a traditional show of affection.

"Glad to hear it," Joe said. "I bet you even keep those fancy English on their toes. And Levi seemed pretty glad to hear you were coming. You know I never told anyone how I saw you sneaking off with him before you left. I was SO jealous."

"I'll ALWAYS be your sister," Kay said. She wondered if she could tell him how she and Autumn traveled back in time to meet Queen Anne. Had her baby brother even heard of English Royalty? That monarch's total disregard for the feelings of others would most likely shock this quiet farmer? Aggressive women never stayed Amish.

Kay gave her baby brother a hug – not an Amish thing – but she did it anyway.

"Have you met Charity and the twins?" Joe said.

"Charity's cool. Who are the twins?"

"Mam's cousin from Iowa died and left them with us to raise. They're makin' hay with Priscilla's man's daudi. Be here soon if not already," Joe said.

"Seems the house filled up after I left. Our mother must not have missed me much," Kay said.

"I was missin' yah though. When I grew up I thought I'd really get you to marryin' me. For sure and certain." He smiled the engaging little boy smile Kay remembered from when he was a child.

"You're something else." Kay hugged him again.

"Awe. Come on now," Joe said. "I ain't missed ya that much."

"Hey Joe." A boy dressed in English clothes strutted up to them as if he were in his running around years.

"That crazy Injun' Jim aint' gonna' hurt no more Amish," he said.

"Eli. Don't go round tellin' that stuff to jus' anybody." A girl who wore her hair down and looked the same age interrupted him.

"Katie," Joe said, "meet your rebellious twin sister and brother, Eli and Elizabeth."

"Ella," the girl said. "Eli talks too much fer his own gut. Gotta learn him some."

"Who hurt Amish people?" Kay said.

"Just a barn raisin 's all," Joe said. "Indian Jim came braggin' about how he helped some of his kin rape those Amish girls in Pennsylvania. They burnt down the barn and everything."

"I read about that," Kay said.

"He aint' doin' it NO MORE!" Eli said.

"I said to shut your mouth." Ella punched him in the chest. Hard.

"It's only our sis," Eli said. He acted as if her hit barely touched his overgrown muscles.

"Our English sis an' ya don't know what she's gonna' go tellin' nobody," Ella said.

"She don't know nothin'," Eli said.

"And she doesn't want to know. Eli," Joe said. "Now you go get yourself some dinner and keep your trap shut. Why don't you?"

Eli wandered to the barn. His shoulders slumped.

"Tell me what it's like to be English and all that," Ella said. "Annie and Andy said that ya drive a car like Levi's an' ya fly in airplanes across the ocean. Ain't ya' scared? Satin being the prince of the power of the air and all."

"I want to know what happened to that Indian," Kay said.

Build That Wall

"Everybody knew what would happen to him the moment he opened his mouth," Joe said.

"Who did it and how?" Kay said.

"Ya' been away too long," Ella said. "We don't ask no questions. There's them that knows 'bout it and there's all the rest of us who don't want no details. Ya see."

A chill ran down Kay's spine.

Her modern world would send a sheriff to investigate and put the man in jail. After tens of thousands of dollars and years of agony the Native American might be put to death anyway.

Even if Kay knew the details what difference would she make?

"But we're supposed to live in peace. We're taught to harm no one," Kay said.

"I'm pretty sure that none of the church members did this," Joe said.

"Ja. Right. And when the sinners join the church all will be forgiven." Kay remembered the sudden transformation of her brother Matthias. He raised a ruckus and fought with their parents until the fall day when he decided to marry his pregnant girlfriend. He joined the church and became a model Amish man.

Kay wished he'd made amends but everyone seemed so pleased to have him in communion with the brotherhood that nothing else was ever said.

Had Matthias ever helped hurt anyone?

Kay's gut said yes.

But the Amish had their own justice.

Did that include letting outsiders take care of Amish "problems?"

"I see your brain runnin' just like it did back then. Ya think too much Katie. Let's get some dessert and eat ourselves full 'fore they put it away," Joey said.

"I was thinking of letting Andy stay with you for the rest of the summer but now I want to get him away from here as soon as possible. What does he know about Indian Jim?" Kay said.

As if on cue Andy appeared beside them. "Was that Uncle Eli over here?"

"Yes," Kay said. "Tell me about him. What do you know about Indian Jim?"

"Did you know that Harley's an American Indian and cousin Autumn is half Indian? Eli's cool. He likes Indians. He had a date with Indian Jim. They were going to meet up with some other guys," Andy said.

"You know what, Andy. You're so grown up. Almost a man." Kay's brother Joe pulled her son toward him and bent down to look into his eyes.

Andy straightened his back and nodded.

"You'll understand that I can't have you staying the rest of the summer after all. Eli may be in his running around years but he can't be coming 'round mouthing off. I need to talk with him 'for he gets us all in trouble."

"O.K. Uncle Joe." Andy's back slumped and Kay wondered at the grown-up sound of his voice.

Joe straightened and spoke in a mater-of-fact tone. "Let's go get you some whoopee pies and ask your Mammi if she'll pack a care package for you to take with you when you go."

"Thanks," Kay said.

"Anything for my family. And don't go makin' yourself scarce now. Write to me all regular like." Joe led her back to the group gathered around the table.

"Andy and I have an announcement," Joe said. "Tonight when his mam leaves she'll be taking him with her. I would appreciate it if the womenfolk could see clear to fill a sack with whoopee pies and whatever you think he'll like."

Kay grabbed her brother's hand in gratitude. "Thanks. I'm proud of you," she said. "Such a wonderful gut father and husband you are."

"Pride's a sin Katie," Joe said.

"I didn't mean it like that. The English translate that word differently. I'm just happy to have such a kind and loving brother," Kay said.

"You're forgiven," Joe said. "'kin I let Andy have one of my pups? He calls my littlest white bitch Merlina, short for Merlin's wife."

"Sure." Kay felt as if she were the mom who couldn't say no.

"I'll go get her ready." Joe turned to the barn.

"Can I come with?" Kay picked up her slice of pecan pie topped with whipped cream fresh from today's milking.

"Sure." Joe led her to the stall and shone his flashlight on a young dog who sat in the middle of her cage waiting as if she knew they were ready to release her.

Joe opened the door. "You get to go home with Andy," he said. "I know that's what you've both been waiting for."

The dog stood to accept her collar and leash. Then followed them to the washing tub.

"We want to make you all pretty for your trip," Joe said.

Kay lit the lantern and grabbed some shampoo while Joe pumped water and caressed it across the suds. Then they both took turns rubbing clean towels over the white fur.

"You're beautiful." Kay couldn't contain the words.

"There ya go. Sinnin' again." Joe spoke in a teasing tone.

"Is it prideful to tell an animal she's pretty?" Kay said.

"I guess not. Least ways since ya aint' got ownership yet," Joe said.

"Not until I sign on the dotted line. After that I'd better watch my ways," Kay joked.

Joe pulled out a drawer from his file cabinet and handed her a paper. "Certified and everything."

"Our folks will have a fit," Kay said. "You giving me this valuable animal. They'll think you have to treat all your siblings the same."

"I only account to my missus and she aint' likely to disapprove. She likes your Andy. An' onct I 'splain 'bout yer' concerns over Eli she'll be glad what I done."

The Amish Time Traveler

"You aren't paying us off, are you?" Kay held her hand over the paper waiting to sign it until her brother answered.

"Nein. Jus' makin' amends fer' any wrongs done," he said. "Sometimes I have't pray pretty hard over some of the things I see. I know how much you want to find peace and I won't judge ya none fer it."

"But you've found your own way to the true ideals of the Amish. I'm happy for you brother." Kay signed the papers. "A true thoroughbred. Man and bitch. Both of you."

Kay knelt to look the dog in the eye.

Merlina seemed to smile.

Kay took the leash and walked to the door.

Joe blew out the lantern and followed her with a flashlight.

Andy ran up and fell on his knees in front of them. "Merlina! I've come to see you. I wish you could come home with me but I have to leave tonight. We must be grown up and not cry."

"I just made a deal with your mam," Joe said. "The dog's yours as long as you write to me every month and tell me how you're all doing."

"You CAN talk English when you want," Kay said. "I bet you get all cleaned up and everything when there's business to be done."

"Shh." Joe laughed at her. "Don't want the secret to get out."

Andy buried his face in the dog's fur and didn't say anything.

"Trying to save face." Kay whispered to her brother. "Just like you did when you were little."

Joe rubbed Andy's hair. "Why don't you and yer bitch spend some time here getting' ta' know each other fer' ya come on up ta the house."

"I love you brother," Kay said.

"An I be lovin' ya too sis'. Can't figure out why ya went off an' left me 'without a word."

"I make some really bad decisions," Kay said. "I was naïve. Uncertain."

"I can't imagine it. I always thought you were ALL grown up and knew everything. That's for sure and certain. But there's this

Build That Wall

Mennonite doctor in Berlin writing about the high incidence of social anxiety and Asperger's syndrome that goes undiagnosed among the plain folks. Beings as how you were always off on that swing of yours keeping to yourself and all, I wondered... Well. If you hadn't come up to me and hugged me I'd have asked you if you thought you had a slight case of..."

Vehicle lights turned down their lane and headed toward the barn. The car's muffler sounded as if it had needed to be replaced about a year earlier.

It sputtered next to Kay and her brother. An ancient-looking woman jumped out.

"Get those twins outta here. Their father's gonna send the law to charge you for kidnapping." She motioned to Andy and his dog. "Where's the girl?"

"Grandma B." Kay wanted to hug the woman.

"I'll get Harley and Annie." Joe took off running toward the food tables.

"Listen Andy." Kay knelt down to her son's level. "Just because your father and I argue doesn't mean we care about you any less."

"I know Mom," Andy said. "Can I leave with Grandma B just in case Dad comes up the lane? He won't recognize her car."

"Sure. You and your puppy can lay down in the back seat." Kay opened the creaky door and watched him hurry inside the car.

"It's gonna be o.k. I won't let my dad get you. He doesn't like puppies but I'll keep you safe." Andy knelt on the floor and cradled his dog on his lap.

Merlin seemed to come from nowhere and jumped in next to them as if to guard them from harm.

"What's up Mom?" Annie walked up to them. "Uncle Joe said you want me."

"Get in here." Andy scooted himself and his dog away from the door. "Uncle Joe gave us Merlina and Dad's going to come and take her if we don't watch out."

Annie crawled next to her brother. "Here," she said. "Put him on the lump between us." She pulled an old Indian blanket off the seat and laid it over the pup as if to hide them.

Grandma B slammed the door closed and the hinges let out a dramatic screech.

"I'll be leavin' then. Tell Harley to meet me at my place." She turned the car around and crept back down the road.

Merlin's head shone from the back window as if he were guarding royalty.

"Was that my Grandmother?" Harley said. "Joe said she wanted to talk to me right away."

"Conrad's on his way here." Kay grabbed the rental keys from her pocket. "Use these and go see your grandmother. Drive the children back home. ASAP. Can you still get into my house?"

Harley nodded. "See yah Cous'. When Grandma has one of her seeings we obey. The truck keys are under the floor mat. I'll call the bed and breakfast soon as I get to your place. My Gramma'll pack up our stuff for us."

He ran to his truck and riffled through a few things... then got in Kay's car and took off.

Kay stood next to her brother and looked up at the stars. They looked bigger... farther away without the city lights.

The normal noises of her family cleaning up after themselves drifted out to her.

"Asperger's syndrome. Huh?" Kay said. "You wonder if I..."

Two cars turned in the lane and drove toward them.

Kay backed to the shadows of the barn to watch for Conrad without being seen. He unfolded his long legs from the Mercedes sportster and walked up to the police car.

She wanted to run at him. Pound him into the ground.

The man CLAIMED he had no money and then bought a brand new luxury vehicle.

"I'd better get down there." Joe strode toward them as if he needed no introduction.

Build That Wall

"Hello Conrad. Officer Dan." His voice rang loud in the night air. Kay felt as if he wanted everyone to hear his words.

The rest of the family conversations quieted.

Conrad seemed confused, as if he were disappointed by Joe's show of peace. "Who are you?" he said.

"Joseph Troyer. This is my farm," he said. "And you must be my sister's Ex-husband."

"I brought her the divorce papers," Conrad said. "And this police officer is here to help me retrieve my children. She stole them from me. Now she'll have to pay me child support. I see her Cousin Harley's truck here so they must be here too."

Joseph turned to Officer Dan. "I wouldn't look for Harley right now. He loaned his wheels to another family member. The womenfolk are just cleaning up the last of the desserts. I'm sure they could dig something up for you while we figure this stuff out."

"I'm not going anywhere until I see my children," Conrad said.

"Relax. If they ARE here we'll find them," Officer Dan said. "They won't be able to sneak past us."

"Family and friends." Joe turned toward the tables to make the announcement. "This man is Katie's Ex-husband. He came to deliver their divorce papers and he wants us to help him find his children."

"That's right," Conrad said. "Kay brought them across state lines without my permission."

"And it only took him several weeks to find out." Joe's voice rang true and clear. "So now he needs the English police department's help to get Katie's children back."

Officer Dan ducked his head away from Conrad as if to hide a smile of respect for his Amish neighbors' sharp wit.

Tension ran through Kay's family so thick that she felt it clear across the lane.

"Wow," Katie's oldest brother Matthias said. "It only took less than a month for you to notice that your own children got stolen! You're one sharp Englishman! But it must be hard... needing a woman to support you with HER money. You really do need our help!"

Kay slipped further into the darkness to swallow a laugh.

Conrad acted as if he didn't even know that these backward farm folk made fun of him.

What shocked her more? Conrad's sleaze or Matthias' defense of her?

In the eyes of the Amish even an Englishman failed when he lost track of his own family!

AND he wanted to shame them for it.

They'd confound him with kindness!

Conrad would NEVER accuse them of anything less.

Mother ran into the house and came out with two huge pieces of German Chocolate cake topped with fresh hand-churned ice cream.

She handed the plates to the two men.

"What else can I get for you?" she said.

"Do you have any coffee?" Officer Dan said.

"I'll make that two." Mother ran back to the house.

One of Hope's boys — Kay couldn't remember his name — sided up to Conrad. "Last time I saw Andy he was over in the barn with the puppies."

"Andy and his mutts. He's always asking for one." Conrad said. "Let's go find him."

Kay scooted inside the barn door and out of sight just far enough that she could hear everything.

From her hiding place Kay saw several of her nephews follow Conrad to the other side of the barn. "I heard someone talk about hunting for snipes," one said. "It's that time of year. Maybe the twins aren't in the barn they might be in the field hunting snipes."

The boy did not tell a direct lie. There were several sets of Troyer twins at the gathering and Levi had mentioned Snipe hunting earlier. But a fudge of the truth by a boy too young to join the church... no one could find fault in that.

Besides, Conrad deserved much worse than being led all over the pastures through cow pies in his fancy shoes.

"Snipe hunting?" Conrad said. "How does that work?"

Build That Wall

Several boys talked at once. "If they aren't in the barn, they must be snipe hunting. We'll help you figure it out."

They led Conrad to their pasture.

Kay sneaked out of the barn and over to the police car.

"He doesn't have a chance. Those children will keep him out all night," Officer Dan said.

"You're right," Joe said. "Curfews and bedtimes for the young'uns have just been unofficially canceled, and I used to think Conrad was smarter than my family."

"You all know that I hated to come here. That man has NO business around children," Officer Dan said. "He brought the correct legal papers and I have to obey the law but I don't have to hurry about it. How much time do you need?"

"I think it might be possible that Katie's children may just be getting out of their own beds around lunchtime tomorrow if they're really slow about it," Joe said.

"That shouldn't be hard to manage," Officer Dan said. "Where is your sister? Does she know if he's ever been on a snipe hunt?"

"She's right here," Joe said.

Kay and the officer shook hands.

Levi appeared beside them, suddenly looking small after Conrad. "If the boys run out of things to do I think I have some business investments Conrad might want to investigate. They're overpriced and low yield but you never know. It could take a day or so before we know for certain."

"I don't suppose Grandma B's been over for a visit recently has she?" Officer Dan said.

"You just missed her," Kay said.

She stepped next to him and shook his hand. "I'm the sister. Kay. My family still calls me Katie. And I'm a big fan of Grandma B."

"That woman's never been wrong that I know of," Officer Dan said. "I'll keep my police radio on. If I get an emergency call I may have to leave for a while but I'll make it back at least by tomorrow noon. In the meantime you may want to check Conrad's car. It sounded a bit rough on the way here. His battery cable may be too tight and I have a suspicion the factory added an extra hose to his radiator that might just be better off on the dashboard."

"You never know with those fancy new engineers," Levi said. "Sometimes they just don't make sense."

Mother hurried down the steps. "I have your coffee," she said. "Where's Conrad?"

Levi turned to Officer Dan. "You go. Take a load off your feet and eat something. I'll fix that problem with the tight cable."

"Aren't cables supposed to be tight?" Mother said.

"Mrs. Troyer." The officer turned toward the house. "I think you make the tastiest German Chocolate cake I've EVER eaten."

"Aww. Now. Don't go makin' me proud," Mother said.

"Just telling it like it is."

"D' you need someone to hold the flashlight?" Kay followed Levi to his car.

"It might be better if you stay out of sight." He lifted a small tool set from behind his seat and walked to the BMW. "Here. Take my keys and get out of here. I'll follow you to Aunt Sadie's when the coast is clear."

"Thanks," Kay said. "You heard Harley. His keys are…"

"I heard him…" Levi said. "Now get out of sight."

"I'll go to say my goodbyes before I head to my aunt's bed and breakfast to wait for news," Kay said.

A wave of homesickness washed over her. She'd missed this feeling of family. Brothers, sisters, aunts, uncles and cousins gathering at an hour's notice for a common purpose of supporting each other with an unspoken intimacy.

Then Kay remembered her twins and hurried toward the house…

Charity hurried up to her. "They say you're leaving. I need to say goodbye. Do I have to call you Katie? I heard that some people call you Kay."

"You can call me Sis if you want. Just don't call me late for dinner." Kay grabbed her sister to her and held on tight.

"Now I have an emergency to attend to. I have to leave. But I will come back to visit," Kay said. "There's a strange English man running around in the pasture looking for snipes. Don't talk to him."

"Can I tell him my jokes?" Charity said.

"NO! No jokes for him! Your family needs them too much. No jokes for the strange English man." Kay looked Charity in the eye to make certain she got the message.

"No jokes for the strange English man. No jokes for him." Charity repeated the words over and over again.

Kay turned to leave but Charity grabbed her arm.

"I have to tell you something Sis," Charity said.

"Kay has to leave before that strange English man comes back," Mam said. "Charity, what did I tell you about talking?"

"Don't never interrupt?" Charity repeated as if by rote. "But Sis don't seem to mind much."

"Charity…" Mam spoke in her correcting voice.

"Yes Mam." Charity pretended to zip her mouth shut and shuffled from one foot to the other as if she were too excited to stand still.

"Well, you may as well go ahead," Kay said. "I can stay one more minute."

"An English man stopped his car in front of our house. One of those camera things he used for our ducks. But his car… it couldn't start. Six aspirins Mam gave him. One for each hole in that box. A battery I think he called it. Then the car. It started right up," Charity said.

"Is that true Mam?" Charity said.

"Ach ja," Mam blushed as if she were embarrassed by a compliment. "Twern't nothin'. We discussed it. Talkin' at the quilting bee. Thought he might as well give it a try."

"Charity," Kay said. "You're the best thing that's happened to this family in a long time."

"'Tweren't nothin'." Charity repeated her mam's words. Blushed and hung her head. "'Sides, 'taint this family. 'Tis our family, Kay. Why you been away so long?"

"I had some things I needed to do but if you get Mother to help you write me a letter I WILL answer it. You need to tell me your jokes," Kay said.

"I write by myself." Charity turned to their mother. "Do we have her address?"

"Harley gave it to us," Mam said. "Get goin' now Charity 'fore that Englishman gets back onct'. I'll give Levi that care package for your children. He can take it to your Aunt Sadie's before you leave."

Chapter 11

Kay had just finished packing the suitcases when Levi pulled up to the curb.

"Get any sleep last night?" Kay said.

"A bit. Officer Dan just stopped by your folks' house to tell us that the Pennsylvania police found your children asleep in their own beds." Levi smiled as if he were a cat with the tail of a mouse sticking out between his teeth.

"I forgot how Amish communication works better than modern technology." Kay laughed and threw her arms around Levi in a hug. "How'd Conrad take the news?"

Levi stepped back. "You're something else! Do you just go around hugging everybody?" he said.

"Sure. Why not? I'm happy. My children are safe." Kay backed up a step. "Tell me about Conrad."

"When I mentioned the price of farmland in these "hicks" of ours he seemed to forget all about his family," Levi said.

"Figures."

"Officer Dan and I fixed him up with a realtor for around 4:00 this afternoon." Levi spoke in his calm farmer voice that modulated the significance of his words.

"I'll be in Pennsylvania by then. Most of the way home at least," Kay said. "I've missed the country ways of this place. The simple intelligence."

Levi let the compliment slide. "Need a hand driving?"

"How long would it take you to get ready?"

"Your mam already fed me. I can go now," Levi said.

That's right. Mother rose before the sun to fix the family breakfast so the men could eat the minute they finished milking the cows.

"Then we just have to say goodbye to Aunt Sadie." Kay led the way back up the walk to the bed and breakfast.

"I hate this truck!" Kay climbed down from the cab of Harley's four by four and stepped on the sidewalk in front of 323 Erie Avenue. She stretched her back. Her legs. "Thanks so much for driving me, though," she said.

"Glad to do it." Levi pulled suitcases from the back – moving as if he still felt refreshed after missing most of last night's sleep.

Kay opened the door to her home and stood back to let him inside.

"I'll just put everything in the front room so you can sort it all out," Levi said.

"I can't wait to see my twins, do you mind?" Kay said. "I'll make some iced tea and we can open that care package when you're done."

"No problem. You need your rest," Levi said.

Kay wondered what he meant but she dropped the subject and felt herself return to the Amish way of caring for and feeding the men-folk.

Oh well. Levi drove her all the way home. He deserved some pampering.

Harley sat at the Formica kitchen table with a man who looked as if he were an older version of himself.

"Kay. Meet my uncle. Eagle Stillwater," Harley said.

Eagle stood and bowed his head in respect. "Pleased t' meet ya," he said.

"Join us for some of my mom's sun tea," Harley said.

Kay sat at the table and let Harley fill her glass with ice, then pour the tea in her glass.

"How come I never met you before, Harley's uncle? And where are my children?" Kay said.

"I'm Harley's father's oldest brother. Me and the girls headed north when Harley was a little tyke but my Edna's daughter is in the hospital. For cancer." Eagle's voice caught in his throat.

Build That Wall

"The girls took your children to the QMart to find some things for Merlina," Harley said. "They should be back soon."

"Is Edna your wife?" Kay studied the man and knew how Harley would look in 30 years if he decided to live in the mountains and earn his way by hunting and fishing.

A thick graying braid hung down the Eagle's back. His skin draped across his face.... The crackled leather-look of a man who spent long years in the outdoors. His kindly eyes smiled over a mouth that missed its two front teeth.

"Edna and Tammy are my girls," Eagle said.

"Oh. Your daughters," Kay said.

Harley giggled. Put his hand on Kay's arm. "Tell her, Uncle," he said. "She's a big girl."

"After my wife died I felt like I'd go right up to the next life with her but then her older sister Edna took me under her wing. She and Tammy and I've been together for nigh on 20 years now," Eagle said.

"And Tammy is her daughter?" Kay said.

"Tammy's Edna's first cousin. The two women are inseparable." Harley looked at Kay and smiled as if he hoped he shocked her.

"You're trying to distract me, young man," Kay said. "I don't know if you two are trying to tease me or if you're telling me the truth but I've been sitting here trying to be polite when I'm so tired I can't even think straight and I want to see my children."

"Hi Mom." Annie burst into the kitchen followed by Andy and Merlina. "Look what Aunt Edna and Aunt Tammy bought us."

Andy dropped a basket on the floor and Merlina plopped down next to it panting from the heat. Andy grabbed a knotted rope from the basket and baited the dog into a half-hearted game of tug-of-war.

"Sit," Harley said. "Everyone sit and I'll get some tea."

The women positioned themselves on either side of Eagle Stillwater. Tammy held up his glass to be filled and Edna patted a stray strand of hair back behind his ear.

Kay felt as if she sat across from two sisters who looked after their precious baby brother.

Levi came in and sat next to her. "Everything's in," he said. "You'll have to sort it out later."

"This is Harley's uncle Eagle and his wives Tammy and Edna." Annie squeezed in next to Levi to make the introduction. "They came down from Maine to see their daughter. She has cancer."

Levi nodded to each of the elders as if nothing were out of the ordinary. "My cousin and I went moose hunting up in Maine," he said. "There's nothing like a white winter morning. The quiet solitude made me feel as if we were the ONLY men on earth. We brought back a bull moose every year for 4 years in a row. Of course that was before I married and settled down."

"I work as a guide during the season." Eagle shook his head as if he were in disbelief. "Those city slickers are something else. One time two men came down the dirt road looking proud as a couple of peacocks with a dead mule strapped to the back of their brand new Ford truck like as if they'd shot the biggest bull moose in the country."

"What'd you do?" Levi said.

"I had 't call the game warden." Eagle shook his head as if in disgust. "Ya just can't go around shootin' somebody's ass. Whatever the law did to those two city slickers it wasn't enough. Coming out from the city harassing poor folks. Killing their pets or even their tractor."

"Hunting season's been dangerous even in Haycock," Kay said. "I never let the kids out of the house the first day of buck season."

"Yeah. One time our dad was on the roof and he heard a bullet go right past his head," Annie said.

"Nothing more dangerous than human stupidity," Eagle said. "Unless it's stupidity with money."

"Uncle Eagle," Andy said, "Don't you think Merlina's just about the best dog you've ever met?"

"A dog aims to please ya young man," Eagle said. "When you took her away from her mama you agreed to take care of her for the rest of her days. She knows that. There's nothing in her life more important than making you happy. Don't you ever forget."

"I won't." Andy answered with the air of a young man swearing an oath.

Kay let out her breath.

She hadn't realized she'd been holding it until now but ever since Conrad had shown up in Holmes County she'd been nervous. Now she finally felt as if she were home. Not with her Amish kin. Not in the house Hilde had given her. But home nevertheless... amidst a peculiar and unorthodox family who cared for her. People who would never even think of fitting into the rules of the Ordnung.

She felt as if her body blended in with the chair.

Her eyes drifted closed.

Chapter 12

"Kay."

She looked up to see Levi.

"What? What's up? Are the twins all right?" she said.

"The twins are in bed. You fell asleep at the table and we helped you to the couch but I thought you'd maybe want to go upstairs to bed before I go to Autumn's for the night. She's offered me her guest room," Levi said.

Kay sat up and looked at the suitcases strewn across the room.

"I should have put this stuff away," she said. "Nothing's unpacked."

"The children dragged some of their things upstairs and put their laundry on the washer," Levi said. "The rest can wait until tomorrow."

"I'm embarrassed," Kay said. "You offered me so much if I married you back then. I threw it all away on Conrad"

She and Harley had cleaned this place. Painted the bedrooms and sanded the floors. But the living room wallpaper looked about 30 years old. Browned and needing to be replaced.

This house seemed so much worse than the one Levi'd built for her in Holmes County. Her furniture looked as if it were on the verge of falling apart.

"It's God's will," Levi said.

"Thanks," Kay said. "But I don't understand you. At all."

"How about you get some sleep in your own bed and we talk tomorrow?" Levi said.

<<☼>>

Kay awoke to the smell of coffee.

She traipsed into the kitchen in her housecoat to find Levi standing at the wood cook stove making pancakes in an electric skillet.

Dishes filled the sink.

Autumn, Harley and the twins sat at the table and Merlina tumbled over Merlin as if he were a toy.

"See Mom," Andy said. "We don't have to buy a new fancy stove for the summer. Levi set the skillet and coffeemaker on top of the old one so it doesn't even make the whole house hot."

Kay had kept the wood cook stove for Andy because he loved old things. He'd fight her on replacing it for sure now that he'd spent so much time with his uncle Joe.

He sneaked a piece of his pancake to Merlina and the puppy scampered behind the stove to devour it.

"I haven't decided what to do about it yet. Don't get your heart set on it," Kay said. She remembered the one in Levi's house in Holmes County. It had been the perfect combination of old and new with a hot water tank and the combination of wood/gas cooking. Maybe she could compromise and buy something along that line.

She poured herself a cup of coffee and sat at one of the empty place settings to add cream and sugar. "Are we expecting company?" she said.

"We invited Eagle and the girls but I don't know if they're coming," Harley said.

"If this keeps up I'll have to get a bigger table," Kay said. This breakfast reminded her of the constant flow of people who came in and out of her mother's house and made themselves at home in Holmes County.

Levi placed two pancakes on her plate and added three slices of bacon. "There's plenty of homemade applesauce, he said. "Your Mam sent some boxes of canned goods with me as a gift."

"Sounds like her." Kay spooned the sauce on her plate and remembered canning bushels of it in the late summer. Nothing from the store compared to the sweet-tart taste of sauce from the apples picked fresh that day.

"Where'd you learn to cook?" Kay said.

"Pancake mix." Levi smiled like a mischievous child. "I learned the basics when my wife was sick."

"I'm not actually sick but I have been tired lately. I don't know why," Kay said.

"A lot's been happening," Autumn said. "Give yourself a break."

"I haven't seen you since we got back from Germany," Kay said. "How've you been settling in?"

"Uneventful. Lots to catch up on. Mostly routine. Pain in the neck stuff but it's good to be home," Autumn said.

"Did my mother send the bacon too?" Kay said.

"Yah. Can't you taste it?" Levi said.

"Nothing like home-grown food." Kay looked around her simple kitchen and felt the goodness of love.

She still missed Hilde but the legacy her mother-in-law had given her consisted of more than things. Her family was connections... the people she loved and who loved her in return.

Happiness consisted of enjoying the now. She'd never found it in seeking the happily ever after fairy tale ending.

At this moment she felt more content than she remembered ever feeling. Maybe Levi was right. Maybe her life was just the way it was meant to be at this very moment.

<< ☼ >>

The twins had gone to bed. Autumn and Harley left for their house and Levi sat across from Kay at the kitchen table.

Her mind flashed back to the beautiful oak furniture he'd offered her before she left Holmes County.

She turned from him and let tears slide down her face.

Who was she? Why did she feel as if she were a 32 year old woman going on 16?

"I'm sorry," she whispered. "If I'd stayed with you... you'd have given me a more stable life. I just couldn't do it. I'm glad you brought me back here but I still don't know if I can do this. Seeing you next to Conrad. You're the much better man. It's just... I don't know."

"It's me not you. Isn't that a line from a movie?" Levi said. "It's too late to start all that stuff now. We haven't had enough sleep. Besides you said you'd make me some tea."

Kay willed her tears back into her eyes and opened the cupboard to bring out a tray of Autumn's dried loose peppermint, chamomile and spearmint.

"Quite the connoisseur," Levi said.

"Autumn shares with me," Kay said. "She grows her own. I'm hoping to learn how to do it if I ever stay home long enough."

Kay put two teacups and a pot on the table.

Levi studied the labeled jars. "Why don't we mix chocolate mint and chamomile?" he said. "Restful before we go to bed."

Kay sipped her brew and let its warmth slide through her body. "We seem to have caught up on some of the main events since we last saw each other but I haven't told you about my summer, how Autumn and I traveled to Queen Anne's England where we found our friend Steve and the three of us made our way south through Menno Simons' Germany and into Austria."

"We may have to change from tea to coffee if the story goes too late but I can't wait to hear it." Levi refilled his cup and held it in both hands as if he wanted to keep them warm.

"Just promise me that if it gets too hard for you to handle you'll stop me before you freak out," Kay said.

"I'm listening," Levi said.

"I have to start by telling you that I've had dreams of a carriage accident all my life." Kay swallowed the sense of dread she experienced around this ex-Amish man. What if he labeled her crazy?

"I'm listening," he repeated himself.

"After I left Conrad I sprained my back and ended up in bed. Harley loaned me Autumn's books on England and I became so enthralled that Autumn and I went to visit.

"Long story short. We ended up at Eden Manor – the deserted property of Queen Anne's niece, Lady Katherine. We opened a box on her dressing table and found an amulet that sent us back to Queen Anne's era," Kay stopped talking to gauge his reaction.

"Keep going," he said. "I'm not the naïve boy you left behind in Holmes County."

"It's hard for me to believe, but I either relived or saw through a life in the past. The amulet took me back to the carriage scene and I actually reversed Lady Katherine's fate. Instead of dying to save her son she kept them both alive. It changed Eden Manor. Now it's a Quaker School for girls."

"It's way outside the Ordnung we grew up with," Levi said, "but when I visited Mennonites in Germany I felt it. I never told anyone this but I felt as if it were possible to time-travel back to Menno Simons' time, to be there and watch history."

"That's what we did," Kay said. "After we left Eden Manor we traveled through Germany to Austria. Now that I'm sitting in my own kitchen it seems so far away. It feels impossible."

"Tell me." Levi reached his hand across the table and held hers. "Tell me all about it.

Build That Wall

Part II
Deutschland

Factoid: *Back to the Future* won eleven Academy Awards in 1985.

Build That Wall

Chapter 1

Kay stood in the drawing room at Eden Manor and stared at Lady Katherine's portrait. Her innocent longings and the shadow of Queen Anne's fool seemed to stir through the room as if they were a breeze.

"A saying for you." The fool spoke in his sing-song voice.

Round and round. Up in a spiral
The seasons and the lives.
A lesson revealed. A lesson learned.
In the journey of a child.

Kay's two lifetimes became one memory. Lady Katherine from Queen Anne's England felt no farther in her past than Katie Troyer's childhood.
She recalled how:

Teddy followed her around the manor helping her inspect the repairs, his attitude of distain replaced with respect.
Katherine read the book on farming and spent Sven's money with Amish frugality. She bought new livestock and designed tools for her blacksmith to forge. She helped Quaker children tend straight rows of vegetables. Pick apples and prepare mulled cider.

Kay let her connection to Katherine fade. The smell of thyme wafted through the open windows.
The fragrance of jasmine.
Lavender.
Rosemary.
"Katherine. It me," he said.

"Are you a ghost?" Kay touched her neck to see if the amulet had sent her back to Sven Nicholson, the handsome commander of Queen Anne's ships and the father of Lady Katherine's son.

No.

The tree still lay trapped in the box.

"I'm quite alive," Sven said.

No. It wasn't Sven it was Steve, the young man from Hellertown, Pennsylvania. She'd met him in Quakertown the Richland Meeting House and he'd shown her the letter from Lady Katherine to his forefather, the commander.

Steve looked true to his style of the preppy student.

"I'm Kay." She looked down at her hiking shorts and reminded herself of the year.

How long since Katherine had seen Sven?

Two and a half centuries?

More.

The math alluded her.

"I'm Steve. Remember? From the Quaker meeting in Pennsylvania."

"Yah." Kay rubbed her temples with her forefingers and tried to equalize the pressure inside her head.

"Glad I ran into you again." Steve's gray-green eyes seemed to read her soul.

Kay recognized the gaze of Katherine's lover back in Queen Anne's England.

Could he have told her the truth? Had they lived other lifetimes together or had they just seen through time to the patterns of life that reflected the lessons they needed to learn in the here and now? But that wouldn't explain why Katherine gave up everything for a stranger.

Kay walked to the couch along the wall.

She sat and tried to orient herself.

"Remember? I showed you the letter from Friend Katherine to my many-great grandfather." Steve sat on the floor in front of her.

"I feel like I've been here before but it was different." He shook his head as if the movement would jar sense into his mind.

"Good word. Different," Kay said.

Surreal.

Impossible.

Inconceivable.

"It seemed like I saw this manor when..." He seemed unable to finish the sentence.

"The school's empty for the summer I presume." Kay tried to remember.

No.

She still felt gaps in her brain.

"I'm with a tour group. We went sightseeing non-stop until we got here. Now we're taking some unexpected quiet time. Isn't it great?" He spoke in a slow voice as if he exerted effort to control his emotions.

"What day is it?"

"Tuesday. July fifteenth."

"Only four days since I got here?" It seemed like two centuries.

Then Kay remembered.

Time is fluid.

Her days in Katherine's body hadn't been the same length as the ones she spent in England.

Steve pulled something from his pocket. "I found a copy of the letter from my ancestor in the library here. Steven Scott changed his name from Sven Nicholson when he fled to America."

Kay's hands reached for it....

For the confirmation of her memories.

"I also found part of Conrad Slater's journal. Enough to show how he believed he killed Sven."

Kay remembered it as if from a dream.

"Katherine got the letter from Lady Hortense. His sister-in-law." Kay patted her sofa.

A Queen Anne piece.

Oh yes. Annie. Was she named for Queen Anne?

The Amish Time Traveler

Andrew – Katherine's best friend and now her son.
Paul seemed to learn his lesson.
Hortense changed when she joined the Quakers.
But Prudence. Would she ever learn?
"The letter and diaries are in order!" Steve said.
Kay felt a child-like thrill pass through her.

She barely knew this man who'd given Katherine a child, that is, if Sven and Steve were the same person.

"I want you and your cousin to travel down to the continent with me. Take a boat to Saxony. Explore Germany and Austria," he said. "I dream that maybe we knew each other in a past life. I see mountains. A crystal cave."

"Thank God I'm sitting down," Kay said. She felt dizzy. As if she were remembering a scene from hundreds of years ago.

Chapter 2

Kay leaned on the rail and gazed across the English Channel. She remembered her flight to England when she watched Back to the Future on the front screen.

She'd considered it a waste of time.

Too fantastic.

But when she and her cousin decided to fly to England Kay felt as if the trip just might help stop the nightmares she'd been having.

Then, stuck in the closed airplane watching the show seemed to be the right thing to do.

"God of our Fathers." Kay had prayed a silent prayer from her childhood. "Show us your way. Lead us in your path."

Autumn had replied as if she'd heard Kay's plea. "Father Sky. Send the Great Spirit Wind to show us the place of memories in Mother Earth."

"Didn't know you're awake." Kay shuddered. Why did she still feel like a heretic around her cousin's unorthodox ways? Autumn never insisted that anyone else accept her beliefs.

What made it so hard for Kay to give up the Amish rules?

"Couldn't sleep," Autumn said. "Besides, it says here that Marty McFly's the only kid ever to get into trouble before he was born."

"I'm surprised you didn't see it yet."

"Didn't take the time. But I'm seeing it now."

Kay watched the ending credits.

Why hadn't she taken the twins to see Marty? In a couple of years Annie and Andy would be teenagers.

Maybe she should travel back in time to spend more time with them.

No. She'd done the best she knew.

Maybe all mothers did their best.

The Amish Time Traveler

Had Cousin Harley taken them to Holmes County?

She hoped the bishop allowed her mother to talk to them. The thought surprised her.

She used to remember her parents with their harsh ways only but surely they wouldn't be so strict to their English grandchildren.

Besides Annie and Andy would want to know their heritage.

"That was fun," Autumn said. "I love time-travel."

Back then Kay had thought it far-fetched — Marty going back to his mother's high school and escaping her romantic advances.

But now....

Now they headed toward Deutschland.

"I wonder what we'll find next," Autumn said. "We're like Marty McFly fixing the past."

Irritation swelled through Kay's chest.

Autumn acted as if she knew so much more than Kay.

Again.

She was usually right, but still.....

"Are you afraid what we might find?" Autumn touched Kay's hand. Then wrapped her fingers around Kay's.

Fear seemed to cloud Kay's thoughts.

"Not just scared," she said. "Terrified."

"Terrified of what?" Autumn gave Kay all of her attention.

"I've made SO many mistakes. I've lost almost everything. Again," she said. "This last minute trip seems insane. Irrational at the very least."

She'd left Levi.

She'd ignored the warning signs before she married Conrad.

What new mistake did she hurry toward?

"Sometimes my own life seems as much of a fantasy as Marty's and I don't like it," Kay said.

"How did you feel when you left Holmes County?" Autumn said.

"Torn." Kay remembered the moon peeking through the new leaves on the trees. The loneliness of rejecting the best marriage proposal she'd ever get.

"And sure." In her heart Kay knew she'd never fit in with Levi's rules. She'd never be able to give him what he wanted. What he needed.

She'd planned to go live with Autumn for over half of her life. If she didn't leave right then she'd have been stuck there. Forever. Well, at least for the rest of her life.

"I did the right thing no matter how painful it felt," Kay said.

"How'd you feel when you married Conrad?" Autumn said.

"By that time I didn't invite you to the wedding because you didn't approve," Kay said. "The real reason may have been because a part of me wondered if you were right. I suppressed those feelings because I wanted to marry him anyway. I felt as if I NEEDED him. I didn't want to live without him. I loved him but I think I loved his mother more."

Tears still came to Kay's eyes every time she mentioned Hilde, the mother she'd always wanted.

"Do you feel that way now?" Autumn said. "Do you feel as if you'd rather be home?"

Kay thought about the release she'd felt when she read Autumn's books on English history. The focus on finding freedom. The sure certainty of doing the right thing. The trip to Eden Manor and how she'd changed her own history.

"No," Kay said. "This adventure feels right. Against every inner voice that cries out to condemn me as a fraud."

Chapter 3

Kay had learned the history of Amish faith from her teachers in the Ebersole School.

A 16th century Catholic priest named Menno Simons left the Catholic Church to marry a nun and live a non-violent life of equality. His followers – known as the Mennonites – refused to baptize their infant children.

In a time when the church and the state were one Brother Menno's actions made him an enemy of the law. Both Lutherans and Catholics hunted these heretics and put them to death.

Fifty years later a Swiss Mennonite bishop named Jakob Amman taught the practice of shunning members who violated the word of Got.

His followers known as the Amish migrated to Pennsylvania and Ohio, then across the country and to South America in search of good farmland.

Each day the Amish lived in the Old German Way of Got they honored the memory of the all the martyrs who paved the way for freedom of religion.

Kay had watched the English teenagers in town with their vulgar ways and scanty clothing.

She listened to their speech and tried to repeat it.

Now she lived in the English world and traveled back in time. Would she and Autumn go back with Steve to see early religious rebels?

Would they find what they expected?

Would they be in for a surprise?

<< ☼ >>

In Bremen, Germany, Steve rented a car at the airport.

"I want to visit Muenster." He pointed the VW South.

"That's not the way we do it." Autumn pulled a goose feather from her purse and attached it to the car mirror. "Great Spirit of the Wind draw us to the place of memories in Our Mother Earth," she chanted.

"God of our Fathers. Show us your way." Kay repeated the silent childhood prayer.

A week ago Kay's plea had been out of fear for Autumn's potential heresy. Now she prayed the request just in case her cousin hadn't covered all the bases.

"Wow. I can feel it. Are you two shamans or something?" Steve said.

"Just two people in search of peace." Autumn settled back in her car seat as if she were a woman on a mission of discovery.

"I know that look on your face," Kay said. "Where's the amulet?"

"Right here in my pocket." Autumn patted the left leg of her walking shorts. "Safe and sound in its ivory case."

"Don't go getting any ideas," Kay said. "Let me know before you get it out."

They'd found the silver tree at Eden Manor north of Oxford in England. When Kay lifted the talisman by its chain and removed it from the box it had transported them back to the time of Queen Anne.

Now it seemed as if the car drove toward Muenster with the same sense of desire as their Mini-Cooper had driven them to Oxford.

What would they see?

Kay's stomach churned. She sensed her fate as certain as if she sped toward her past and future both at the same time.

"I bought a tourist book at the airport." Autumn held the tome up for Kay to see in her seat behind Steve.

"I can't read in the car," Kay said. "I get dizzy."

"Muenster. Home of the Muenster rebellion," Autumn read.

The Amish Time Traveler

Kay felt her body tighten. Nothing her Amish ancestors had taught her mentioned the city of Muenster, yet she felt the power of its significance deep in her bones.

"In 1535," Autumn continued to read:

> ...followers of the Anabaptist radical – Melchior Hoffman — expelled the unsympathetic citizens from the city of Muenster. They condemned the meek non-resistance of evangelical martyrdom and instituted their iron rule of communal living.
>
> A tailor named Jan Matthias anointed himself as the new King David. He established polygamy, renamed their city the "New Jerusalem," and instituted martial law.
>
> More than a year later Prince-Bishop Franz Von Waldeck broke through their fortresses and found most of his subjects starving and broken-spirited.
>
> On January 22, 1536 Prince Bishop Von Waldeck gathered his allied princes to view "King Jan" and his two assistants, Bernhard Krechting and Bernhard Knipperdolling where they were chained to stakes in the public square. Guards tortured them with flesh-ripping tongs for more than an hour before they thrust daggers into the heretics' hearts.
>
> The remains of the three anti-heroes were each placed in a cage and hoisted to the spire of the city cathedral as a warning against any future heretical revolt.

Kay felt as if she were racing toward a strange and familiar past — not the same as her trip to Oxford. Less personal and more historic. As if she knew the past first hand and it had affected her in the same intense way as her own family history.

She felt the grueling violence. The visionary certainty. The sacred knowing of right living regardless of the cost.

The space in time during Menno Simons' writing.

Someone close to her had known this life.

Build That Wall

Someone had suffered.
And escaped.

Martin Luther's Bible: For centuries Catholic priests translated all Biblical texts. The development of the Gutenberg Press and the resultant printing of the German text brought reading to the masses resulting in freedom of thought and the Protestant Reformation.

Chapter 4

When Steve drove through the city gate Kay felt as if a dark cloud descended upon them.

"I don't like this!!!" Kay groaned. "Not at all!"

"What do you see?" Autumn spoke in her excited voice, as if Kay were on a voyage of discovery.

"The women and children bring rocks to fortify the walls. They sing as if they cannot feel the pain in their bleeding hands. But they jail themselves inside. If they try to escape, they won't be able to," Kay said.

She heard them sing the song an echo through the centuries...

> Build that wall
> Make it strong
> Keep us from heresy.
>
> Build that wall
> Cleanse us from sin
> Prepare for Christ's return.
>
> Build that wall
> In Jesus' name
> Help us live for God.

Build That Wall

Women and children made up verse after verse of the hypnotic song.

Kay felt bile rise from her stomach. She covered her ears against the feeling of impending and un-named doom.

"Is she alright?" Steve said. "I'm waiting to park. Should we leave? Get out of here?"

"Don't worry," Autumn said. "She sees through time. She must be watching the Reformation."

"I'm fine!" Kay felt irritation well from within herself.

"Just give me the amulet." Kay reached her hand and Autumn placed it inside. Kay slipped it in her shorts' pocket. "I don't want any surprises."

Back at Eden Manor Autumn had retrieved it without warning.

Things had all turned out.

But still....

The suddenness of it all had been exhausting.

Kay felt the energy of the past rise up around her.

Bernard. Bernard Rothman.

She felt the name. One of her ancestors had known the man. He'd been a theologian and savior to two young girls named Anna and Hester. They'd helped build this wall around the city to trap themselves inside.

Kay stumbled from the car and walked to the bookstore.

Her hand went straight to a little red book on the sidewalk-table. She flipped to the inside page and found the English translation of Rothman's writing:

Jesus is. Was. And always will be the answer to every one of our needs.

These are the days of a new Reich – the reign of the kingdom of God here on earth. Our Lord and Savior Jesus Christ is coming here to Muenster to bring the 1000 year reign of peace to all who believe in him and to all who are baptized through immersion into his spiritual realm.

Prince Bishop Von Waldeck is unfit to rule. He has turned his heart from the one true Got.

The book slid from Kay's hands and she felt her strength melt from her body. The scene in front of her changed to the past.

"Repent!" The preacher named Brother Bernard yelled from the cathedral steps. "Be baptized. Be immersed in the water of the spirit that your old life may be destroyed and you may emerge as a new person in Christ Jesus our Lord and Savior. For God's Kingdom is come here on earth. Prepare for his Reich here in Muenster."

Poor people in rags sat at his feet.
Rich merchants set up tables to sell their wares.
"Make way! Make way for the coming of your Prince Bishop Von Waldeck. Make way!" A crier called through the streets.
Women and children pushed toward the shop walls as fast as they could. Two Belgium horses decked in bells with red velvet ribbons plowed through the crowd careless of any obstacles.
A ragged toddler escaped his pregnant mother's grasp and ran to the middle of the road.
"Johannes! NO!" The mother screamed and ran after him.
The toddler acted as if he played a game of tag and laughed at his mother's distress.
She ran to bring him to safety.
Kay wanted to divert her eyes but she stood still, riveted to her vision.
Whap! Thump! Bump! The carriage wheels caught and kept running. Screams of pain came from the toddler's mouth, then were stopped by the gurgling of blood.
The group of Anabaptists surrounded the mother and child.
"The woman was a baptized true believer," the preacher announced. "She and her innocent child will rest in the arms of our savior this very night! The Bible says, 'Woe unto him that harms

even one child.' Our Prince-Bishop lives in wealth, enjoying the lust of his flesh with his mistress while his wife languishes alone. We have just witnessed his murder of a woman and her two children – one in the womb and one already born. We must rise up and join in the community of believers to share our wealth in the manner of the early church. We must usher in the new Reich of this New Jerusalem as is written in the God's holy and infallible scriptures!"

"What's happening?" Kay heard Steve ask her cousin.
"She's having one of her visions. If we can find a quiet patch of grass, I'll stay with her while you explore," Autumn said.
"What do you mean, she's having a vision?" Steve said. "I thought she only saw through time with the amulet."
"This happened in Oxford," Autumn said. "Sometimes she sees a short scene without any preparation. It's different than when we use the amulet. The amulet could send all three of us back through time to relive an entire section of history."
"I want to stay. See what happens," Steve said.
"Nothing happens right now except she seems to go into a trance," Autumn said. "You can help me get her out of the way, then you can see the sights you planned on. I have this tourist book I can read. She'll tell us what happened afterwards."
Kay felt them loop her arms, one around each of hers, and lead her to a cool shade where they leaned her against the trunk of a tree.
Kay let her mind wander back to the preacher.
He couldn't be a follower of Menno Simons.
None of the plain people even voted!
They worked out the kingdom of Got on this earth within their own communal church. They separated themselves from the world and its politics.
Kay felt her body slip onto the grass and her trance took her back to the Second Reich.

Time seemed to speed ahead.

The Amish Time Traveler

The walls appeared strong and sure. Its gate looked as if it had been permanently closed for years.

The preacher stood next to two of the girls who had helped build the wall. They seemed to have aged into their teens.

"Hester," the man said, "If our king decides it's Got's will for you to become his fourth wife I pray that you will obey him as a Godly and obedient woman. Otherwise I'll marry you myself. I must have a wife and you are too old to remain single

"What about me, Uncle Bernard?" the younger girl said. "Will he ask me to marry him too?"

"You are too young Anna," the preacher said. "You haven't had your courses yet."

Something about his demeanor indicated that he seemed pleased with the idea that younger girl would stay unmarried.

Kay felt as if she would gag.

A putrid smell rose around them.

The smell of a dead animal along the fence row.

Exaggerated by a thousand.

Or a thousand thousand.

A man shuffled past them with a woman on each side. One carried a baby and the pregnant one held the hand of a young toddler.

What was wrong with them? Why did they move as if each step seemed hard?

Their cheeks appeared sunken. The toddler tripped and just lay there as if he were too tired to move. His mother bent down to pick him up. She wiped a smudge of blood off his knee and trudged after her two companions.

The preacher and the two girls watched them go.

"I'm afraid the New Jerusalem is not working out as we had planned. The true believers starve while our new King David has more than enough food for all of his wives," Uncle Bernard said. "You'll be well taken care of, Hester, as long as you don't do anything to anger him. I'm working on an alternate plan for your sister."

"I'll do what you say," Hester said. "But if you ever find a way out of this place you must take my sister and me with you."

"You saw what happened to the people who tried to leave. The bishop's forces wouldn't let them through their lines and they starved to death," Anna said. "And appealing to the king is suicide. We watched him behead his wife just because she asked him for more food for the starving masses. I can't believe we actually built these walls to keep the enemies out. Now we've trapped ourselves inside."

"I will fear no evil." Hester quoted the Psalms as if she were trying to soothe herself. "Death has no hold on me."

"I plead for your forgiveness," the preacher said. "Our Brother Menno Simons was right. I've been very wrong for working toward the second Reign of God here on this earth. Our Lord and Savior Jesus Christ calls us to a non-political life of love and caring on this earthen-home."

Kay watched the scene drift away.

She let herself slip into an empty space as if the light shone on her. Washed the horrors away from her.

"Time to find some rooms for the night. Steve's here." Autumn nudged Kay on her shoulder. "Can you walk or do you need help?"

"Just get me out of this place?" Kay propped herself up one arm at a time. "I don't like the energy here."

"Are you caught back in the 1500's?" Autumn said. "Your amulet's still in its case. I didn't open it."

"I went into a trance. The preacher and his... his nieces." Kay rubbed her head. "God, I'm tired. I think I can walk to the car. Can you stay next to me in case I get dizzy again?"

"You saw Bernard Rothman? Tell me about it!" Autumn stood next to her.

"You have to wait. You know that." Kay struggled to her feet.

"I'm not trying to pressure you," Autumn said. "I hoped this seeing-through-time thing would get easier by now."

The Amish Time Traveler

"It is easier than Oxford," Kay said. "It's just... the starvation. The devastation. Even the Prince Bishop. It was horrible!"

"And we thought we had a bad childhood." Autumn led her to the car.

Yah. Kay thought.

She should NEVER complain again!

Chapter 5

Steve turned the car south on the Autobahn.

Autumn touched the feather. Then read from her tourist brochure. "Prince Bishop Von Waldeck borrowed heavily for his war to retrieve his city from the Anabaptists. He died heavily in debt from feeding his many soldiers for the siege, many of whom died along with their families. After the war these fighting men plundered the city for their wages. Famine ensued."

"Enough!" Kay said. "I saw it all. Families starving. Babies. Pregnant women! It was awful. But the followers of Menno Simons believed that the kingdom of heaven is a spiritual kingdom. I've never been so proud of my heritage. We were led by a brilliant man! I have to concentrate on that and get away from all this death."

"It says here that Hitler took some of King Jan's ideas to form his Third Reich and that the early communists used those same principles," Autumn said. "Tell us. What'd you see?"

"At first it was the guy the girls called Uncle Bernard preaching. He sounded like our Amish bishops when he called for a life of purity faith. Then it became militant. Confusing! How can people read the words of Jesus and decide to go to war? Jesus preached peace. Love."

"You guys are cooler than I thought you'd be," Steve said. "You actually SAW Bernard Rothman and the girls who called him Uncle! Wow!"

"If we find a room we can see the results of the third Reich on our way to Austria," Autumn said. "One of the camps isn't far from Munich."

"Sounds like a plan," Steve said. "Do you think Kay will be all right? Do you think she might slip back in time again?"

He sounded excited, as if he hoped she might see more.

The Amish Time Traveler

"NO! No Third Reich for me! I've seen enough walls for one day," Kay said.

She leaned her head back against the seat and willed herself to rest. They wanted her to see two Reichs in two days. What were they thinking?

"I've always wanted to drive on the Audubon," Steve said. "No speed limit. Next time I come I'm driving a Porsche!"

"Why don't we stop at Tauberbishofsheim on our way?" Autumn said. "That's where Kay's mother-in-law lived before she came to America."

<<☼>>

By the time they drove over the bridge and parked next to the river Kay felt strangely rested.

They walked up the cobbled street rimmed by old buildings on each side – stores with a residence built either behind or above the business. A rack of traditional dirndl dresses sat in front of one shop. Shoes in front of another. People sat at the tables next to eating places and drank their coffee or tea.

As always Kay felt drawn to a rack of books and found a map of the Romantic Strass or the Road of Romance – beautiful German countryside filled with trees and streams. Well-kept houses.

"This is more like it." Steve looked over her shoulder. "It's what I'm looking for."

"I've had enough talk of Reich and kingdom plans for a lifetime. I'm trying to imagine Hilde when she lived here as a child. She said that she fell into the river. Her older brother was supposed to watch her but he turned his back. A neighbor saw her dress floating down the current and pulled her out of the water."

"You're not going into another trance are you?" Steve looked at her as if he were examining her mental health.

"That only seems to happen when I return to a place that has special historical significance to a past life. This place is significant to my ex-mother-in-law," Kay said.

She glanced over to Autumn who seemed to be absorbed in the book section.

"I'm done in here. Are you?" Steve walked to the door.

"Can I help you with anything?" The store keeper spoke in broken English.

"How about this?" Kay handed her an English-German translation book. "It should come in handy."

She paid for her purchase and followed Steve out the door into perfect summer weather. They sat at a table and Kay ordered German Apple Cake while she tried to imagine how Hilde had experienced these streets.

"Did you see that crooked house?" Steve pointed to a square three story dwelling with no more than three small rooms on each floor. It leaned toward the hill with several feet difference between the top and the bottom.

"I wonder what holds it up." Kay said. "It's probably historic or something."

"I like the feel of this place," Steve said. "When Autumn gets out we can ask for the Stein Bakery."

"I'm just glad to finally be at the place my ex-mother in law talked about." Kay took a deep breath, inhaled the atmosphere of her surroundings.

Hilde's parents had bought her a ticket to America where she would be able to buy food, a precious commodity in post-World War I, and something Kay had never experienced in her sheltered farm existence.

Kay tried to imagine sending Annie and Andy across the ocean to another culture with the hope of freedom and safety. She couldn't.

Menno Simons seemed like a great prophet, preaching against centuries of war that bankrupt their governments and starved their children.

"Earth to Kay," Steve said. "Where's your mind?"

"I was just trying to imagining how Hilde's parents felt when they sent their youngest daughter away knowing they'd never see her again," Kay said.

"There's Autumn." Steve jumped from his chair. "Let's go see if she found the Stein Bakery."

"Just up the hill on the left," Autumn said. She bustled out the door with a bag of books in her hand.

"Did you buy out the whole store to put next to the urn?" Kay said.

"I found some fun stuff to add to my collection." Autumn's eyes twinkled as if they held a secret and Kay remembered the day she first came to Quakertown.

She'd stood in Autumn's windowed room and reached out to touch the vase on the fireplace mantle.

"That's my husband's urn," Autumn had said. "He always told me I'd never make it on my own. I keep him there so he can watch me."

16 years later she still bought fliers and books from her travels to place next to the urn and remind the long-dead man how well she thrived without him.

"You're something else," Kay said. "Just when I think you've settled down you surprise me again. Hasn't he been gone long enough?"

Autumn just smiled that you do your thing I'll do mine smile and started to walk up the hill.

"There it is. On the left," Steve said.

Small. Non-descript.

Not the huge deal Hilde had fashioned it to be.

The sign. Stein's Bakerie.

No bells. No whistles. No time-travel.

Kay walked up to the door and entered. "My friends and I are here from the USA. My mother-in-law, Hilde Stein, was born here."

"Nien English!" the woman said.

Kay tried her Pennsylvania Dutch.

"Mein Mutter-in-law." Kay retrieved her German-English dictionary just in case her dialect made no sense.

"Hilde Stein," she said. "From USA."

Build That Wall

The woman nodded, then brought forward a man who looked eerily like Hilde. "Conrad," the woman said. "Conrad Stein."

She motioned for Kay and her friends to sit, then she went to the phone.

Kay looked around the room. The place seemed large for an old bakery! The exposed old beams appeared sturdy rather than ornate. Booths looked welcoming. Basic and friendly.

The clientele seemed to be leaving for the day as if the place were almost ready to close. The bakery display seemed empty.

A young woman bustled into the room.

"Hi. I'm Anita," she said. "Conrad's sister-in-law."

"My Pennsylvania German dialect's pretty rusty. I guess I didn't make much sense. But I'm so glad to finally see the place where my mother-in-law was born. She felt more like a mother to me than my own. She talked about this place all of the time," Kay said.

Anita turned to the owners and spoke Kay's message.

"Hilde loved her older brother Conrad SO much she named her son after him too," Kay tried to keep the disappointment from her voice.

The room felt unfamiliar.

In Oxford she knew she'd been there before. Driving through the roads to Eden Manor seemed like traveling through memories.

For some reason Lower Saxony felt familiar.

She'd experienced the history in Muenster first hand – the religious war – the starvation.

But the state of Bavaria seemed strange.

Unfamiliar.

She felt as if she should have felt a stronger connection to this birthplace of Hilde's.

If only she could relieve herself of the blank feeling.

The disconnection.

As if she'd never been a part of this land.

Maybe Kay's heritage was the love of kindred spirits instead of a geographical place.

The Amish Time Traveler

Maybe Autumn. Hilde. Grandma B. Her crazy neighbor with the dogs on Erie Avenue in Quakertown. Pearl from Eden Manor constituted her true heritage.

Kay and Hilde shared a connection to their home in Haycock but the Stein Bakerie in Tauberbishofsheim was Hilde's alone.

The German Conrad served them coffee and cake while Anita chatted about the area. "Why didn't your husband come with you?" she said.

"My cousin and I were in Oxford and finished up early so we decided to drop down to Germany before we went home. We met our neighbor Steve while we were there and he decided to come with us," Kay said.

"It was nice meeting you," Steve said. "I think I'll check out more of the village. It's got some nice history." He walked out the front door.

Kay felt at a loss for words. She looked at Autumn wondering if her cousin could help her.

"You've been very kind." Autumn held out her hand in farewell. "It's been wonderful to see where Hilde lived. It's helped us see her as she was. If you're ever in Pennsylvania please feel free to visit us."

Kay followed Autumn's lead, shaking everyone's hands before leaving the restaurant.

They met Steve near the top of the hill.
"I need to see the Catholic Church," Kay said.
She walked inside and stared at the stained glass windows.
Angels.
The Virgin Mary at the annunciation.
Elizabeth and John the Baptist.
Kay marveled at the mixture of men AND women included in the artwork.
Of course most of the feminine likenesses seemed subservient. Then Kay remembered Hilde's story:

Build That Wall

When I was a child I almost died. The Priest came and prayed for me and I lived.

It was a miracle!

This strange town.

Kay could almost feel the anger from its last war. Could it be the place of miracles?

She looked at the statue of the Virgin.

The face of Jesus.

She walked over to the candles and lit one, then dropped a Deutch Mark in the box.

She crossed herself for the first time in her life and bent on one knee.

"Let there be peace," she said.

Let there be peace for memories of the past and for discoveries that lay ahead.

She turned and walked back out of the door where Autumn and Steve studied the architecture.

"Ready to go," she said. "Or do you want to see more of this place?"

"I'd like to drive down the Romantic Strass," Steve said. "I wanted to go all the way to the Austria we've all dreamed about. I thought I was into this WOOWOO stuff but you kind of freaked me out in Muenster. Let's just drive south and enjoy the scenery."

"Then let's go," Kay said. "And we can skip anything to do with the second or the third Reich. The walls around concentration camps and the one through Berlin didn't seem to work much better than the one around Muenster.

Chapter 6

Kay grabbed the wheel until her knuckles turned white.

She'd taken her turn at driving and they'd lost track of the roads an hour ago. She decided not to ask for directions.

Awhile back they'd stopped to have their passports checked to enter Austria. Now they climbed a narrow winding road.

The mountain rose to their right – up out of sight.

A barrier of steel posts and eyebeams seemed to provide an insufficient protection from stray rocks that might decide to crash down onto the road.

Tall pines surrounded them and jutted toward the sky as if drawn by reverse gravity.

The mountain dropped straight down on their left.

Kay felt afraid to look. Ferns covered the woodland floor on both sides, interrupted by an occasional cluster of wildflowers.

The aroma of crisp mountain air and fresh pines filled the car.

She drove around an abrupt curve. A stream tumbled down the right side of the mountain, cut under the road and came out on the far end.

A lump of emotion erupted from her belly and lodged in her throat.

A large building rose before them. Flowers flowed from window boxes. Painted Bavarian scenes decorated the exterior. Tables and chairs sat on the patio for outdoor dining.

Kay felt as if she remembered this lodging house... or an earlier version of it.

"Ffernpass-hotel." Steve read the sign out front. "This is such a great place. Let's pull over and stop for lunch."

Kay turned to the back seat. "Autumn. You can wake up now."

"Let me sleep." Autumn unhooked her seatbelt and snored.

Kay climbed out of the car and starred at the *zimmer* sign.

Then wandered around the side of the building.

She stared at the remnants of what appeared to be a built-in animal shelter that had been converted into a garage.

An ancient BMW and some bicycles stood in front of it.

Kay stared at the structure.

A strange foreboding welled within her as if it were connected to hidden night terrors.

Unreasoned.

Unexplainable.

She half-expected a burly man to crash through the door and threaten her.

"I know what you mean," Steve said.

"Did I say something?" Or had he read her mind?

"I saw you looking," he said. "It must have been where they kept a cow in the old days. But it makes me shudder. As if it holds a secret."

"You're right. I can feel it," she said.

"It's been here for hundreds of years. We don't have history like this in the states," he said.

Was he trying to divert her from the past?

"Just think what it would have been like to live here then." She spoke more to herself than to him.

"I don't know," he said. "I can see you living in a place like this. Your nickname would be Pepper."

"Pepper? You say."

"Yea."

"Let's see. And I suppose that if you lived here I would call you Steffi."

"Austria's an old country. I'm sure there must have been more than one Steffi in the town's history." He looked at her and smiled.

How was it possible for his gray-green eyes to get more intense each time she saw them?

"How does it feel?" she said. "Taking on a new identity and all."

"Interesting. Younger." He seemed to ponder a moment. "Actually it doesn't feel like a new identity at all. When I'm with you everything feels natural and comfortable – as if it always was and will be."

"I know what you mean." Kay's body gave a visceral reaction to this inn that seemed as familiar as Holmes County, Ohio.

"Anything's possible here," Steve said.

They walked towards the building.

"Why don't we get them to pack us a lunch and so we can hike some of these foot paths up through the mountains? I bet we'd have a great view." She pointed at a break in the trees.

"Yah. I wonder if the restaurant is set up for picnics," he said.

They entered a large waiting area that reminded Kay of the lounge in an old tavern. To their left a dining room opened onto a patio furnished with tables and chairs overlooking the valley below them.

"You two ran off without waking me up!" Autumn charged into the room and let the door slam behind her.

Her hair stuck out in four different directions.

She looked as if she were exhausted. Kept upright by sheer adrenalin.

Kay recalculated her plans. "We wanted to let you rest while we took a hike. But since you're awake why don't we eat outside on the patio?"

Kay glanced over at the car and felt as if her mind played tricks on her.

Everything seemed to be in order but this place called to her soul as much as if her feet had been planted in the rocky earth.

Her lungs sucked in the cool pine air.

But she sensed unrest.

An evil-presence just around the corner.

It could hurt them and take their car.

"Beautiful," Autumn said.

"Just like Eden Manor," Steve said. "We've been here before. Do you feel it?"

"What do you think, Kay? Is it near the place where our tree-dreams take place?" Autumn appeared to study Kay's face.

Kay turned toward Steve and felt truth in their connection.

"Tree dream?" He kept her gaze.

She felt her insides tumble.

"Would you like to be seated?" a waiter said.

"Sure." Kay felt as if he'd rescued her from a panic attack.

"I'll have a beer along with your pork and sauerkraut," Autumn said.

"Along with a large dose of gas." Kay smiled.

Chapter 7

After they rented rooms for the night Steve took off for a walk while Kay and Autumn wandered past the ancient church building to the ruins of an old cottage.

"I can feel it in my bones," Autumn said. "Can't you?"

Kay nodded. She took silent measurement of her sensations.

Comfort.

Good memories.

Followed by terror.

"Take out the amulet," Autumn said. "Please."

"You're always in a hurry." Kay pulled the ivory case from her pocket and removed the silver tree. The shiny green setting sent vibrations through her and she felt time lose its grip.

Suddenly she felt as if she could see back into the early 16th century and karma showed her each person's thoughts in this village center.

It was the year Arabelle turned twelve.

The Pope reigned supreme as the ruler over life and death of all his subjects.

<< ☼ >>

Arabelle helped Mam remove bread from the village bake oven when soldiers seemed to appear out of nowhere.

"Orders from the bishop." The giant who dressed in a bright red uniform sat on his white steed in front of a half dozen of his followers. He held up a paper full of terrifying marks, then motioned to his men.

Two of them dismounted.

"Captain of the Swiss Guard." Mam whispered.

Arabelle stared at the giant. Her tongue froze in her mouth.

Build That Wall

The captain pulled a long knife from his side. It shone fierce in the midday sun.

"It's a sword," Mam said. "Don't move."

Mam kept a kitchen knife in the pocket on her apron.

Pa used a scythe for harvest.

But Arabelle had never seen such a blade.

The captain pushed the tip of his weapon to Mam's throat until he backed her to the oven.

"Obey me. Or she dies." The sound of his voice sent a shudder through Arabelle's body.

She watched his eyes scan the crowd while his two soldiers traveled through the group forcing each woman to remove her headdress and bare her neck.

"You want me." Mam unfastened the silver pendant from around her neck and held it high.

Arabelle recognized the heirloom. It had been her mother's mother's passed down in the tradition of the women as far back as Zipporah – the wife of Moses. According to tradition it had appeared at the bottom of the burning bush after the fire stopped.

The captain stared at the Tree of Life.

The length of a small hand, the amulet resembled a woman's body whose hair rose as if it were the branches on a sprawling oak.

Pure crystals adorned its tiny leaves.

An emerald heart.

Pink Ice.

Purple. Amber. Scarlet. Indigo Blossoms.

A garland of tiny pearls wound through its branches.

The soldier tossed the only treasure of the village to his captain who dangled it from his fingers.

Arabelle watched the sun dance a rainbow of color through the stones.

She wondered if the captain served the Pope or if he fed his own greed.

"I alone follow the old ways," Mam said. "No one else."

Arabella wondered what Mam meant.

The Amish Time Traveler

Everyone in the village came to her for their illnesses. Even the village priest knew how Mam traveled to the crystal cave to meet an ancient woman before each solstice.

The father once told Arabelle that Mam "is the kindest and most Christian woman in the village. He encouraged everyone to visit her for advice and treatments for their ills.

"It is forbidden." The captain eyed Mam as if he tried to assess the truth of her words.

Then he lifted his sword.

With one swing he sliced off Mam's head.

The blood gushed up from her neck. Her body crumpled to the ground.

Arabelle fell on her knees and burrowed her head in her mother's chest. Warm sticky blood oozed across Arabelle's face.

Her hair.

Her body.

"There is one God." The man pressed the broad side of his sword on Arabelle's skirt and wiped the blood clean. "Our most honorable and holy pope hears God's voice alone. You must keep no sacred relics for yourselves lest you be driven into heresy."

Arabelle looked up to examine the soldier's evil eyes.

How could he speak of God?

She grabbed Mam's body and wailed.

"Quiet!" The captain ordered. "Or you're next."

Arabelle's body stiffened.

She felt as if she were paralyzed.

"Padre." The captain shouted. "This infidel will not be given a Christian burial."

"Search the rest of this hovel." The captain kicked his horse to action knocking women and children to the ground as if their lives mattered nothing to him.

<< ☼ >>

Tears ran down the face of the village priest when he said the sinners' prayer over Mam.

His face looked pained when he followed the pallbearers who carried her body to the field reserved for unbelievers.

Arabelle and Pa stood alone to mourn Mam's passing.

Their friends had stopped by the cabin to swear secret support and Pa had begged them to stay away from the public burial lest soldiers come back to find them disloyal to the Roman Church.

Chapter 8

After the funeral Arabelle walked as if she were in a dream. She followed the stream where it rose above the village and up the mountain as if she were in a trance.

At midafternoon she came to its source where water spouted from the carved mouth of the face of a bear on the side of a cliff and created a cool pool before tum*bling down the mountain rocks.

An ageless woman stood beside a small beach. "Do you call that captain an evil man?" she said.

Arabelle ignored the question and sat on the grass to remove her shoes.

She dipped her feet in the cold depths and wondered if she'd ever feel good again.

"Call me Pearl." The ancient woman dropped Mam's amulet on the ground next to Arabelle. "The soldier knows not what he does. This belongs to you and to the women who follow you."

Arabelle reached out to touch her mother's treasure, fearful lest the captain come back and slice off her own head. But the silver tree seemed to jump into her hand.

"Keep it for the one who comes," Pearl said. "This treasure chooses her own keeper. The soldiers do not understand."

"He's evil. That man," Arabelle said. But she felt the power of the amulet flow through her and question her understanding.

"Truth survives," Mam had always said.

That's why she stood in front of the soldiers without fear.

Was there something Arabelle missed?

"Evil – I do not understand," Pearl said.

"Neither do I," Arabelle said. "The captain's heart must have shriveled like a prune. How else could he enjoy lopping off my mam's head?"

"Your mam would have claimed that he hurt others to quell his own pain," Pearl said.

"I'd like to cut his head off." Arabelle wondered if she spoke the truth. She'd rather eat roots and herbs than cut apart a chicken.

How could she kill a man?

"That's what your mam meant." Pearl spoke as if she read Arabelle's thoughts. "She is a wise woman."

"Was. Was a wise woman." Arabelle collapsed on the ground and sobbed.

How could she go on living without her Mam?

"Her body joined the earth," Pearl said. "Nothing more."

"But I can't see her. I can't hear her." Arabelle screamed at the old woman. How could she BE so dumb?

"Your mam lives in your heart where you will find the answers you need," Pearl said. Then she walked into stone cliff – which felt more logical than the rest of Arabelle's day.

The young girl laid on the earth until she felt the sun move toward the horizon.

Then she followed Pearl's path toward the rocks to see if she could figure out how Pear disappeared. She reached toward the cliff and watched her hand disappear into the earthen colored aura.

She stepped back and looked around.

Nothing seemed extra weird so she walked forward and pressed her head through the glowing illusion.

Pearl sat cross-legged in the middle of the crystal cave bathed in a rainbow of lights.

Arabelle joined her.

The sun shone straight in her eyes.

She turned in a half-circle until it warmed her back and bounced rainbows of light all around her.

A gentle breeze tugged her hair.

Played a hypnotic tune on the walls.

Arabelle held Mother's amulet to her chest and felt its vibrations transport her back to the moment the soldiers appeared in the village.

This time she saw their hollow haunted souls under the rich red and blue uniforms.

The Amish Time Traveler

When her mother's blood sprayed in the air a muddy tormented face erupted from the commandant's chest screaming in agony.

In contrast Mam's spirit rose from her body in a beam of light so bright that it seemed to release her to new life.

Arabelle brought two crystals back from the cave. She hid them under the rocks in front of her cottage and waited for the prophesied one to come and claim the amulet.

Each season for forty years Arabelle traveled up the mountain to visit Pearl and celebrate the old ways of her mam.

She earned the name Oma Ara – the oldest woman in the village – by the time she placed her youngest granddaughter Katie on the ground next to her foster son Theodoric Steffen.

Toddler Katie grabbed the stone with both hands.

She pushed it aside and pulled out a dirty crystal as if she knew what she sought. Her foster brother scooted beside her and grabbed the other rock.

They stuffed them in their mouths.

Held them to the sun to make rainbows.

Then banged them together to make noise.

Katie smiled at her Oma Ara as if she knew the importance of what she did.

Tears filled Oma Ara's eyes.

Two children. Male and female. Complete.

She willed herself to live long enough to see the babies memorize the ancient ceremonies.

<< ☼ >>

Every spring solstice Oma Ara led the two children to the crystal cave.

They washed colorful rocks in the spring pond. They prayed to the God of Love whom the Popish church called the Holy Spirit even though they seemed to have forgotten that part of God.

Build That Wall

Theodoric Steffen or Thor's mam had died in childbirth and his father sent him to live with Oma Ara in her the weaver's addition to her son's and Katie's father's shepherd's cottage.

The fall before they turned twelve Katie and Thor held the amulet to the setting sun and watched the sparkling rays shine through the jeweled branches to form a rainbow above them.

When they returned home Thor's father took him home to live and declared that forever after his son must be called Steffen after the first Christian martyr.

Katie went home to her grandmother's bed to sleep.

Throughout the long winter evenings Katie sat with her older sister Pauline and listened to their mam tell the story of her life while Papa smoked his pipe and polished his tools in Oma Ara's attached room.

By spring Katie and Pauline could recite the tales with as much emotion as if they'd lived their mother's life.

Chapter 9
Katie's mamma Anna's story
Muenster 1535

Your Oma Ara is right, Katie's mam had said.
The popish church got so corrupt that they forgot the true purpose of Jesus.
Love.
Forty years ago a priest named Father Martin Luther prayed all night and drove himself all day to help the members of his parish.
His bishop worried Father Martin would break down from exhaustion so the bishop sent Martin to visit the Pope to find spiritual guidance.
But when Father Martin saw how the head of the church wore jeweled velvet and brocade silk to host drunken orgies and lavish feasts served on plates of gold Father Martin felt betrayed.
He remembered his village.
He saw each child who died of starvation.
He recalled pious parents who dressed their children in rags in order to pay their church taxes.
When Father Martin came home and watched a child die his heart wrenched. How could he serve these church leaders who stole the food from children's mouths to feed their own lusts? How could he help his pope empty the pockets of the poor for his own greed?
When the pope decided to renovate of St. Peter's Basilica in Rome and sell indulgences to raise the money Martin Luther felt incensed. He wrote a letter condemning corruption and demanding 95 reforms to the church.

Build That Wall

He nailed the letter on the door of Castle Church in Wittenberg just like any other priest attaches public notices on our church's doors.

Normally change comes slow.

The paper would have been discussed for years.

But the printing press changed everything.

A German printer copied his demands into the common language and distributed them.

The Vatican condemned Martin Luther for heresy and put a price on his head.

<<☼>>

Martin fled for his life and married an ex-nun. They lived in hiding for ten years while he translated the Bible into the common language of German.

When common people read the Biblical descriptions of Jesus and his love rebellion spread like fire.

The Vatican declared that everyone who accepted Martin Luther's teachings must be put to death for heresy.

But some people were so poor they felt as if they had nothing to lose. They would gladly die a martyr's death and be admitted to heaven rather than starve.

Another group of protesters felt as if Luther should have gone farther. They read that John the Baptist only preached to believers. Therefore babies remain without sin until they reach the age of consent. Baptism must be reserved for people who are old enough to DECIDE to commit their lives to Jesus Christ.

The pope responded with rage.

If babies escaped baptism how would Rome collect their taxes?

So the Vatican decreed that all heretics MUST be tortured for at least an hour – so they'd repent and turn their hearts to the one true God before they died.

Sheriffs created wheels to stretch people's limbs from their bodies and special harnesses for horses to pull people apart.

The Amish Time Traveler

They hung people by their thumbs and used hot tongs to pull the flesh from their bodies while they watched.

They beheaded and quartered the dead bodies – hung the pieces around the city as an example for all to see.

Vultures and dogs fought over the remains.

But the number of converts to the new baptism grew larger.

Whole families sang in ecstasy when sheriffs led them to their deaths.

They cried to heaven while flames burned them alive.

So the Catholics cut out their tongues and blindfolded them to keep the crowds from seeing their joy.

For every one who died two converted to take his place.

Crowds cheered and praised God for release from the evils of Popery.

A group of believers declared themselves the ONLY true followers of Jesus Christ. They reasoned that since Jesus was baptized as an adult only adults should be baptized. They called themselves Anabaptists.

An Anabaptist scholar named Bernard Rothman traveled through Anna's village and took Anna and her sister Hester with him to Muenster. The excitement seemed contagious. For the first time in their lives the two young girls had more food than they could eat.

They felt as if they lived like princesses whom God had rescued them from poverty and death.

Prince Bishop Von Waldeck sympathized with the Anabaptists but Uncle Bernard wanted more.

When Von Waldeck barred Uncle Bernard from spreading his heresies in the St. Lambert's Cathedral Uncle Bernard moved outside to the steps.

Great crowds came to hear him every day.

Chapter 10

"We answer to a higher calling greater than any ruler of this world. We answer to God and to God only!" Uncle Bernard preached.

"Amen!" A wealthy cloth merchant called out. The rich fabric of his robe shone bright in contrast to the ragged beggar who stood next to him.

"Our pope would have us baptize babies. Newborn and unable to answer God's call on their lives. These infants cannot account for their own actions. Jesus calls us to repent and be baptized in his name. He calls us to make an informed decision to follow him. Therefore we MUST be baptized as ADULTS! How can we accept ANY earthly power which forbids us to follow the commands of Jesus? The pope claims to anoint his own rulers but the lustful and gluttonous Prince Bishop Von Waldeck lives in open adultery with his wife AND his mistress."

Anna sat on the steps next to her sister behind Uncle Bernard and watched when a young man sidled up to her.

"What's the name of this preacher," he said.

"Bernard Rothman. You must be new to Muenster," she said. Everyone knew her uncle.

Well... not everyone.

But his enemies had already left the city.

"My name's Jan," the stranger said. "Jan the tailor."

Anna nodded in acknowledgement.

"Stay. Enjoy Uncle Bernard's sermon," she said.

"In Revelations we read that Jesus is coming back to institute a second Reich or kingdom in the city of the New Jerusalem. His followers will rule and reign with him. In this new Reich there will be no giving and taking of property. Everyone will live without need just like in the book of Acts where the deacons in the early church collected the property and distributed it as there was need. No one went without."

"That would be an improvement," the tailor Jan said. "I come from the Netherlands where the rich get richer and for every weaver with a job there are two whose families are starving."

Anna knew that story.

Her own father had lost his job.

Then her parents died.

Along with her baby brother.

"On my way to Muenster," Uncle Bernard preached, "I came upon a place where famine and pestilence took everyone's life except for two young girls. These youngsters came with me to the New Jerusalem. They left everything behind to follow Christ."

He turned and motioned to Anna and Hester.

"Stand up, children," he said.

Anna felt shy. Unworthy next to her sister.

"Will you follow Jesus?" he yelled.

"Yes," they both said.

"I can't hear you," he said.

"Yes!" Anna screamed. "I will follow Jesus!"

She hated being in front of people but she knew her uncle. If she and Hester didn't cry out he'd just keep calling on them until they did.

"Amen!" Tailor Jan jumped up and screamed. He threw his tattered hat on the ground. "Alleluia Jesus!"

Something about Jan made Anna's stomach wrench but she tried to ignore it.

"Our Emperor Charles has ordered his soldier to kill those of us who accept adult baptism into the kingdom of God," Uncle Bernard preached. "They put us to death without inquisition. But Jesus says, 'What can it profit a man to gain the whole world and lose his own soul?'"

"Amen!" Tailor Jan jumped up and danced on the steps of the cathedral.

Anna scooted from him and inched away.

Build That Wall

A nun swooned in front of her and cried out in a strange language.

Jan grabbed her hands and yelled as if he were translating her words. "For I say unto you, what does it profit a man to gain the WHOLE WORLD and LOSE his OWN SOUL?"

"Amen. And Amen." People yelled their approval.

Two sister nuns surrounded Jan and started to speak in other tongues.

"Anna," Uncle Bernard said. "Anna. Don't sneak away. Come here and testify. For the woman Eve tempted Adam to sin but through the Virgin Mary Jesus was born into the world to save us from the fires of hell. You are only a child of twelve years but when you are old enough to marry you must come under the protection of man to be saved."

Anna knelt on the steps at Uncle Bernard's feet.

"Tell them how Jesus saved you," he said.

"When death came to take my family," Anna whispered.

"When death came to take her family." Tailor Jan stopped dancing long enough to repeat her words in his theatrical voice.

"I saw Jesus. He sat by my bed and I crawled on his lap," Anna said.

"Jesus sat on Anna's bed and said, Let the little children come unto me just the way he talked in the New Testament. So Anna crawled onto the lap of Jesus himself." Tailor Jan's voice carried across the village square.

"And Jesus' eyes were kind. His robe was soft and warm. Then I knew everything would be all right," Anna said.

"She sat on Jesus lap. She looked into his kind eyes. She felt his soft and warm robe and knew everything would be all right. Isn't that so Brother Bernard Rothman?" Tailor Jan finished Anna's testimony with a flourish.

"Praise the Lord," the nuns chanted in unison.

"Thank you, Jesus." Tailor Jan grabbed their hands and danced in a circle with them.

Someone pulled out a mouth harp and started a tune.

Another man brought his accordion and stamped his foot in time.

"Christ our Savior is calling us to reign with him for a 1000 years in the New Jerusalem," Uncle Bernard shouted. "Will you answer his call?"

"Amen!"

"Alleluia!"

"Ja!"

"Thank you Jesus!"

"Thank you Lord!"

"We will follow you!"

Anna felt the joy around her... not the quiet peace of her visit with the soft man named Jesus with the kind eyes, but the excitement of her uncle and the tailor named Jan.

The entire square seemed to fill with a glow.

"I will follow you, Jesus," Anna whispered. "I will follow you wherever you lead me."

"Our citizens are forced to support eleven monasteries and nunneries. These Catholics sell their food and their cloth at the market driving down the prices the poor citizens of Muenster can receive for their own hard-earned goods. If we refuse to pay our taxes to the Roman Church we go to prison by Papal decree." Uncle Bernard called to the streets from his perch on the steps of St. Lamberts Cathedral.

This time Anna hid behind the crowds and joined a group of women who carried jugs of food to the village square.

"Hurrah," someone cried.

"Praise the Lord," cried another

"There shall be singing and dancing in the streets," preached Uncle Bernard. "For the city of the New Zion."

"Amen. And Amen," yelled the people in the square.

Suddenly everyone seemed to be working together. Some brought tables to the streets. Some brought meat or bread from their larders.

All seemed to be sharing what they had.

Build That Wall

Anna had never seen such love.
Such hope.
Such purpose.

Chapter 11

Anna served tea in their dining room when the Dutch tailor who seemed to double as an actor came to visit Uncle Bernard. Jan seemed to try to memorize every word Uncle Bernard spoke.

"We need to institute true New Testament community living where everything is held in common and no one goes without basic needs," Uncle Bernard said. "We will invite all of the other Anabaptists to join us in our Holy Experiment. We'll call it the Second Reich. The kingdom of the New Jerusalem."

A knock at the door interrupted them.

"Get it Anna," Uncle Bernard said.

"For Bernard Rothman. I must deliver it myself," the messenger boy said.

Anna let him inside and he set the letter on the table. He bowed. "Sir," he said.

"Stand tall," Uncle Bernard said. "We are all equal in the sight of God."

The boy seemed to walk a little straighter when he left.

"From our brother Menno Simons," Uncle Bernard said. He turned to his visitor. "I've invited him to join us!"

"A good Dutchman. A true follower of Christ," Jan said.

"Pssaww." Uncle Bernard tore up the letter and held it to the flames in the fireplace.

Anna had never seen his face so red.

"He claims that God's kingdom is NOT of this world but in our hearts! Jesus calls us to peace, not to war." Uncle Bernard seemed to spit out the words in disgust.

Anna wanted to retrieve the letter. To read the rest of the writing that seemed so true to the Jesus she'd met. She wondered why they needed to burn the written word.

Build That Wall

She slipped out the kitchen door and went to visit Helle Simons who lived next door.

"Have you ever heard of a pacifist priest named Menno Simons?" Anna said. "Uncle Bernard just tore up one of his letters."

"He's my husband's brother," Helle said. "Don't tell me he's condemning us again. Peter will be so embarrassed!"

"I wouldn't worry about it." Anna sat at the table next to her friend and patted her hand. "Everyone seems to have a relative who causes trouble... everyone but Hester and me that is. We don't have any other family."

"You're lucky. Menno's been such a critic. He wrote Peter last week," Helle said. "Peter tore the paper in little pieces. Threw them in the dung heap where they belong."

"Doesn't Menno believe in the New Jerusalem here in Muenster?" Anna said.

"The shame!!! Peter's own brother writing all this heresy. He claims that the Kingdom of God is in our hearts only. He says that war is killing. We must live in peace with all men." Helle put her head in her hands and cried. "I have to do something!!! Anything."

"But we're women. You've heard the preachers. Our job is to help our husbands. To marry and have children," Anna said.

"What are you two talking about?" Hester walked in the door and interrupted them.

"Menno Simons' letters," Anna said. "Helle's embarrassed. Menno is her husband's brother and she thinks people will judge her for Menno's actions."

"That won't happen," Hester said. "Peter is a godly man, true and faithful to the truth of the Anabaptist kingdom of God here on earth. Don't be sad."

"But there has to be SOMETHING I can do to make up for Menno's unbelief! His heresies!" Helle said.

"Let's think. The women in the Bible. How did they help the Kingdome of God here on earth?" Hester paced back and forth, then settled and seemed to study the air.

"Let's consider the women of the Old Testament," she said.

"Sarah married Abraham and became the mother of a nation," Helle said.

"That won't help here," Hester said.

"The King married Esther and she saved the Israelites from the gallows," Anna said, "but I don't think that's what we have in mind."

"Deborah led the Israelites in battle," Hester said, "but I don't think Jan will let you do that."

"Judith conquered the enemy king all by herself," Anna whispered. Excitement swelled her heart.

All of the chosen women of Zion had helped fortify Muenster's city walls.

When the bishop's trained warriors attacked them even the young girls threw pitch and burning necklaces onto the grown men to turn them back.

Anna studied Helle.

Her long lashes.

Skin as clear as the sky.

Shapely body.

No wonder men followed her and tried to grant her every wish.

Helle WAS A SOLDIER OF GOD! HE went before her to set the new Zion free by the hand of a beautiful woman – like Judith.

Anna waited.

Hoped.

She watched Helle grab one of Preacher's pamphlets from the mantle.

"Judith! The story of Judith!" Helle jumped up and down in holy joy. "Judith saved her people by herself!"

She read:

And they escorted her to Holofernes, the leader of Nebuchadnezzar's army.

The leaders of Israel have led me into error, Judith said. Only your God is the one true God.

Build That Wall

Not only are you beautiful but your words are wise. Never has there been such a woman as you. Come and dine with me, Holofernes said.

But my maid has brought our food that we may eat only plain fare and pray for three days, Judith said.

So Holofernes invited her into his tent and each morning Judith arose and bathed in the stream and prayed to the one true God.

The third night Holofernes held a banquet in Judith's honor and he became quite drunk. In the middle of the night Judith grabbed his sword from the posts of his bed and cut off his head.

She called to her maid and stuffed the head into the food bag and went out to pray as she had the previous nights.

When she came to the city walls the guards marveled at this thing God had done for them by delivering their enemy into their hands.

"I'm willing to give my life for God's just cause." Helle stood and paced the room as if her brain mapped out her every move.

"I'll need the permission of all the preachers but they should understand. My husband's brother accuses our city of blasphemy," she said. "I must remove this blot from our name in the heritage of the Godly women of the Bible. God placed me here to save our people."

"Never has there been a more beautiful woman for the job," Hester said.

Anna studied her neighbor's face and a chill shot through her body. This plan felt wrong. It made her heart race in fear. What had happened? Where was the peaceful presence of the man called Jesus?

She forced the idea back inside herself.

"I'll do it!" Helle said. "I'll wear silk and precious jewels. The bishop's forces know that we live in plainness and simplicity so they won't suspect me. They'll believe my lie. I'll tell them I've abandoned the cause because I miss wearing fine things and they'll escort me right to him."

"I've watched you," Anna said. "Wherever you go men follow you and heed your every wish. You cannot fail."

Anna swallowed the nagging fear back in her gullet. "You can't fail," she repeated herself.

She wondered who she tried to convince.

"Tell the bishop you want him to rescue you from the horrible Anabaptists," Hester said. "He won't be able to stop himself from helping you."

What if they failed?

"You know it's dangerous," Anna said. "You could die and we'd never see each other again."

"Until we meet in heaven where Jesus will reward you for your bravery!" Hester stood and raised her hand in the air with the sign of victory.

That was the goal, to live and DIE for the sake of God. Nothing else mattered.

Anna set her teeth in determination. "Let's grab each other's hands and stand in a circle like we do in the market square," she said.

The three girls danced around the room and sang verses from the Bible:

I will sing unto the Lord
For he has promised victory
The horse and rider thrown into the sea.

The Lord our God
Our strength and song
He has become our victory... y... y...

I will sing unto the Lord
For he has promised victory...

Anna felt as if it were the happiest moment in her life.

Chapter 12

Jan appointed twelve Dutch deacons just like they did in the New Testament.
One deacon for meat.
One for blankets.
One for grain.
And so on.
These men came around to each house and collected everyone's possessions to store in the common warehouses.
People gave what they had with joy trusting in the goodness of the one true God.
A couple of months later Jan's deacons brought soldiers to search for hidden supplies that reportedly hadn't been turned in.
Jan preached that no one must keep a secret! ALL true Christians MUST share EVERYTHING in common. Neighbor MUST turn in Neighbor. Brother should tattle on brother. Friend on friend. Children on their parents. No one should hoard private and secret rations.
All this time Hester and Anna heard nothing from Helle and her efforts to replace Judith.
Then one day the guards called everyone to the marketplace. "A martyr," Jan yelled prancing around the stage. "Helle Simon, the new Judith who died in the name of Jesus, gave her life for the new Zion. Great is her reward in heaven!"
Jan bowed as if he were in holy reverence to God.
The cheers arose in unison, "Thank you Jesus."
"Praise be to God!"
"Alleluia."
"Blessed be the name of God."
The hymn:

A mighty fortress is our God,
A bulwark never failing...

Tambourines. Mouth harps. Accordions seemed to appear from nowhere and people danced in circles to celebrate the goodness of the one true God.

How could they be so happy? Anna missed her only true friend. When she walked back home with Hester she saw a light in Peter Simons' window. The shadow of a woman shone against the curtains.

The two girls crept into their house. Tiptoed to their shared bedroom and tucked themselves under their featherbed to whisper about silly stories from their first days in Muenster...

The euphoria of defying the pope.

Their first baptism of the Spirit of the New Testament.

The early days of the uprising.

When they built the wall.

Back then they'd each felt true brotherhood with the others.

They remembered the Bible story of King David's sin and the death of his son.

Moses and the exodus.

And the thousands of Lutherans who came from far away to join their cause. It seemed as if God brought Jan to Muenster as surely as He brought King David to rule over the Israelites.

"Why does it feel as if something's wrong about this whole thing with Helle," Anna whispered under the covers.

"I don't know but you have to keep your thoughts to yourself," Hester said.

The two girls whispered under their covers until the sun peeked through the cracks in their wall and guards pounded on the door of Peter Simons' house.

The girls rushed to the window to see what happened.

"Can you ask the deacons to supply me with another blanket?" Peter Simons' wife said.

Anna stared at her.

Build That Wall

How could Peter have found another wife almost as beautiful as his first one?

"You have a husband to keep your warm." The guard pushed the woman back into her house.

"Just one more blanket," the woman pleaded.

The guard yelled into the house. "Peter Simons. Are you home?"

Peter stuck his head out of the upstairs window. "Yes. May I help you?" he said.

"Keep this woman warm and under control lest she be heated by the fires of hell!"

"Get back in the house, woman!" Peter ran to her and shoved her behind him. "Do NOT cause problems. I'm warning you!"

After that Peter's new wife seemed to disappear. Until the day of the big play, that is.

<< ☼ >>

Later that day the soldiers knocked on every door and asked for books.

"Everything must be burned," they said. "Everything but the Bible and your uncle Bernard's writings. Bring them to the market square before dark."

<< ☼ >>

The fire rose in the air.

Another party.

Women threw themselves in the streets covered with pig dung. Danced. Sang the Psalms.

"David danced naked before God," Uncle Bernard preached. "When his wife laughed at him he cut her off."

"Amen," Anna said. She felt as if someone was watching her and she needed to agree but she couldn't feel the truth of her words.

The emotion seemed out of tune.

Anna loved books! Surely they couldn't all be sinful.

After that night Anna read the Bible every day. She felt as if she wanted to understand all of the sermons she'd heard... to know if they lined up with truth... to see if Jan and the preachers translated their words into practice.

Uncle Bernard spent more and more time in his study writing pamphlets to convert more followers.

When the storehouses of food seemed low a group of citizens asked to leave the city.

Hester and Anna went to the walls to watch. King Jan's troops escorted them through the gates and locked them. But the bishop wouldn't allow them through his lines.

Parents pleaded with the bishop holding their wee children up asking for mercy.

They turned to the soldiers in Muenster and repeated their plea.

The girls watched parents cut the grass out of the ground, they were so hungry. Then they seem to get sick and Anna felt overcome with a new smell. The smell of death.

"The smell of the infidels who turn their hearts from God," King Jan preached.

Hester and Anna tiptoed back to their house and whispered under the covers. "The Bible speaks of love, of compassion," Anna said. "Where is our Christian mercy?"

"Shush... Don't let ANYONE hear you say such a thing." Hester put her fingers to Anna's mouth to emphasize the words. Anna had never felt a more serious plea from Hester.

"It's true," Anna whispered. "God is LOVE!"

"Truth is what King Jan says it is!" Hester said.

Anna studied Hester's features and saw a stern new look on her face. Anna wondered what had caused her to succumb to such a mean spirit.

"King Jan has instituted polygamy!" Hester said. "Just like in the old testament... like King David."

"What's that got to do with us?" Anna said.

Build That Wall

"He used Uncle Bernard's sermons to claim that EVERY woman would need a husband. Because there are more women than men EVERY man NEEDS more than one wife," she said. "Every woman NEEDS to be fruitful and multiply!

A shudder ran through Anna's body.

Every woman!

She'd just started her courses and none of the men knew yet. She might be spared. But Hester….

Hester was 15 years old.

"Uncle Bernard asked if you've had your monthly cycles yet. I had to say yes. Nothing is secret in our world today," she said.

"You're right," Anna said. No wonder her sister had changed so much. She'd watched people starve to death. Now she feared they'd be separated in marriage.

Nothing seemed sacred but King Jan's visions.

After that Anna hid in the house and read her Lutheran Bible. She only went out when King Jan ordered. She wondered how this New Jerusalem improved on the Papist rule.

Muenster had rebelled to gain freedom but now it seemed as if everyone needed King Jan's permission to make their every movement.

She couldn't find any relief.

When the bishop sent his professional soldiers up the wall, she'd been trained to pour hot tar on their heads. Now the screaming dead soldier haunted her dreams. Any sleep she sought ended in terror.

<< ☼ >>

One morning Uncle Bernard woke the girls early.

"You are both commanded to come with me to the cathedral to become my wives within the hour," he said.

He didn't look Anna in the eye.

"What will we call him?" Anna said to her sister.

The Amish Time Traveler

She refused to let her emotions surface. Uncle Bernard had saved them from death but now he forced his ways on them.

"Husband, I should think," Hester said.

"Well we can't call him Uncle anymore. And the name Bernard alone sounds too informal. Do you think he'd let us call him Preacher?" Anna said.

The title sounded much more formal.

Less endearing.

It set him apart while giving him the respect he apparently felt was due him.

"Preacher," she said. "I like it! But we'll have to make him think it's HIS idea."

"At least we'll still have each other." Anna wondered at the truth of her words.

She felt a new distance between herself and her sister as if they were part-strangers and a pieces of them had hardened and died with the starving refugees.

Hester had wandered through the streets these last days…. Always watching.

Anna still felt loyalty towards her.

And she knew Hester reciprocated.

But the true sisterhood. Had it had been lost?

They took turns washing themselves and combing each other's hair in silence. They dressed in their only unpatched dresses and the Preacher led them to St. Lambert's cathedral.

The Dutch deacon read the Psalms, a romantic poem in this place of death. Then he read the passage about the wedding feast where Jesus turned water into wine.

They filled out papers.

"Congratulations," the Dutch deacon said. "It's about time you took some wives Brother Bernard."

"For it is written, be fruitful and multiply." Preacher spoke the command.

Build That Wall

A bolt of terror shot through Anna. She lowered her eyes in what she believed to be the proper manner of a married women and wiped all emotion from her face.

She glanced at Hester and saw a permanent-looking hardness enter her expression. Then each girl took one of Preacher's arms to walk out of the building and down the steps.

<< ☼ >>

Anna had watched chickens shake their feathers after a rooster moved on to his next hen but even so, the females in the village stock seemed to encourage their mates to mount them.

Her own mother and father had seemed to enjoy themselves under the covers. Other than that Anna knew nothing about the marriage bed.

After they came back to the house and ate a small lunch of bread and lard Preacher said, "Do you have any errands Hester?"

"Certainly." She walked out the door as if she knew what would happen next.

"Come to my room wife," Preacher said.

Anna followed him trembling with the realization that he and Hester both knew something she didn't know.

Inside the room he started to undress while she stood by the window and looked out at the street.

"Close the curtains and take off your clothes." His words felt as if they were a command.

Anna felt clumsy when she sat on the bed. She took of her shoes, then covered herself with a blanket while she slipped off the rest of her clothing before she slipped under the covers.

She glanced at Preacher.

He stood before the side of the bed with his member erect and at eye level.

Terror shot through Anna.

She felt as if the world stopped.

"You are my wife! Remove the covers," he said.

The Amish Time Traveler

She could not move.

He grabbed the blanket and tossed it on the floor.

She tried to cover herself.

"You wicked daughter of Eve! You MUST submit to your husband," he said.

He grabbed her hands and pinned them on the bed next to her head and then he jumped on top of her.

She felt her body respond to his hardness between her legs.

"You sit all pious reading the Bible every single day. Do you not read where it says that the husband is the head of the wife? Do you not know that a woman is saved through her obedience?" he said.

His foul breath flooded her face.

She felt his member rub between her legs and a strange pleasure crept up through her belly.

"Do not refuse me!" He commanded.

She wondered how his beliefs could be true to the gentle Jesus from the Bible while she closed her eyes and forced her face to appear peaceful. She tried to make her body relax lest he read her mind and turn her over to the executioners.

He rubbed between her legs over and over until she felt warm and moist. Then he took one of his hands and helped himself enter her an inch at a time..... As if he knew she felt tender.

Her body responded to him against her wishes.

And suddenly he shoved himself inside!

She cried out in pain.

"Shut up you wicked daughter of Eve." He pushed himself harder and harder but her body felt as if it were welded around him.

"You're too tight," he swore. "Why are you trying to keep my seed from giving us children?"

He grabbed her hips and pulled himself away from her and then pushed back inside. His thrusts felt vicious!

She willed her mind to leave her body. To relax and get this trial over.

"That's better," Preacher said.

Her insides felt moist again.

Her body had betrayed itself. Again... as if it enjoyed Preacher's final release.

"That's better," he said. "We'll have to do this every day until you give me a child."

"May I have a blanket now?" She whispered.

She suddenly felt cold.

How had her own mother ever stood for this kind of treatment? How could a loving God want this for any woman?

"You must stay where you are. Let my seed take root." Preacher patted his covers around her as gently as she'd ever seen him.

But she hated him.

Hate was a sin.

She didn't want to sin.

How could her body betray itself so?

How could...?

She let her mind wonder.

Would she ever get used to this wife business?

Would she EVER find the happiness her parents seemed to enjoy?

Her mind quit asking questions.

Calm overtook her.

She entered the place of no feelings.

Then memories of ecstasy.

Victory over the bishop.

Dancing in the streets.

The bonfire of books.

Hunger.

Nothing mattered.

She stared at the ceiling without seeing.

Beams shone. Beautiful.

Nothing wrong.

Her surroundings faded yet they remained unmoved.

<< ☼ >>

The Amish Time Traveler

Anna awoke to the grey before either dawn or sunset. She cared not which. Hester sat on the side of her bed.

"Come downstairs," she said. "Preacher said."

Anna felt detached... as if she were in a dream.

Was this the feeling of silence the prophet talked about in the Old Testament when he said, "Be still and know that I am God?"

The ominous silence seemed to envelope her. Her body removed her feather cover and she walked to the door.

"Come back," Hester said. "You need to get dressed. It's winter."

Something in the back of Anna's mind nudged her into knowing that Hester was right. Anna would be cold.

She turned around and laid back on the bed to let Hester pull Anna's socks up to her knees. Lift Anna's shift over her body. Finish dressing her and lead her downstairs.

A strange girl sat at their table.

"Sister Anna, this is Sister Clara," Hester said. "She's engaged to Preacher. Her mother brought her to live with us until she's old enough to marry."

"Hello Sister Clara," Anna said. Thoughts flitted through her brain without the normal emotions attached.

Maybe Hester wanted the young woman to share Preacher's bed... so they'd each get an extra night off. Or maybe Hester wanted to replace Anna....

But the young girl seemed slow... as if her brain developed wrong.

It didn't matter.

Nothing mattered.

"I have a joke," Clara said.

"We could USE a joke around here," Hester said.

"Let me close the curtains first," Hester rose and checked the street for spies.

Clara began her tale:

One of the bishop's sons decided he wanted to find a wife and he says to his papa, "I like Rebecca and I want to marry her."

"You can't go marryin' her," the bishop said. "Ya see, when her Mam and I were young we went to went out dancing and one thing led t' another and Rebecca's your relations."

A couple a' months later the young man says to his papa, "I really like Sarah and I wanna be marryin' her."

"Well, ya see," Papa said. "Ya can't be doin' that. When her mam and I was young we walked out together and one thing led to another and Sarah's your relations."

The same thing happened with Sadie so the young man went to his Mama and tattled to her.

"Don't listen to your Papa," his mama said. "He aint' your relations."

Clara smiled as if she'd just pulled off the biggest tale of her life. "Ya like it?" she said.

"Do you have any idea what the joke means?" Anna said.

Clara got a puzzled look on her face. "Relations is when you aint' livin' in the same house. Like when you're livin' far away. Aint'?"

"Something like that." Anna smiled at her. Leaned down as if to tell her a secret.

"You can always tell me any jokes you hear. Don't ever be afraid to tell me anything. I won't be upset with you," she said.

"Mam told me to don't never tell nobody," Clara said. "But I knew you was different. You aint' bad even if you are Bernard Rothman's wife."

"Yes. I am his wife." Anna sighed. "Why would that be bad?"

"Aint' you upset with me... tryin' to take your place?" Clara said.

"You can take my place any time you want," Anna said. "I don't think you're bad at all. I like you just the way you are."

"That's why I brought her here," Hester said.

For the first time that day she looked relieved.

"Let's get this place cleaned up for dinner," Hester said.

"I like to sweep the room with a glance," Clara said.

"This might work better." Hester handed Clara a broom.

The citizens of Muenster weren't allowed to lock their doors so they kept them open a crack. Anna felt the damp chill seep into her bones... she never felt warm... even under the feather blanket.

One evening before they finished dinner Dutch guards pushed their door open and yelled, "Your king hath need of you. In the square. Now."

The three girls threw on our cloaks and followed Preacher to the new platform their king had just covered in gold cloth.

A Dutchman who called himself a prophet had broken through the bishop's lines and anointed Jan in the line of the Old Testament kings.

"A display. For your enjoyment." Jan called to the crowd.

Half a dozen Dutchmen came to the top of the steps dressed as monks.

Anna's heart sank.

Would they reinstitute popish rule?

"The Holy Roman Catholic Church would have us believe that all salvation comes from their sacraments and from them alone," Jan — the new King David said.

The monks set up a table in front of the cathedral and layered cloths upon it. They added a chalice and Catholic tapestries.

"Watch as they perform the Holy Catholic rituals," King David announced.

The monks pantomimed filling the sacramental cup with wine... then they jostled to see who could drink the most.

Some wine spilled.

Some dribbled down their chins.

The monks seemed appalled. Then they pretend-fought over the chalice.

"How important are your duties to the pope?" King David said.

Build That Wall

As if on cue the monks turned their backs to the crowd and pulled up the backs of their gowns showing off their soiled rear ends.

"Dear citizens of the New Zion," King David said. "Papal sacraments have no more importance than these monks."

The monks bent and exposed their rear ends one more time.

The citizens of Muenster laughed.

Six months earlier the entire city would have roared with glee. Danced in the streets.

But their bellies had seen too little food on this evening.

Laughter took too much effort.

"Amen," a Dutchman yelled.

"Amen," Preacher cried out.

"All we need is a heart pure toward God," King David yelled

"Our Honorable and Holy King David," a man called from the crowd. "My youngest wife has refused me in my bed three times! It is causing unrest and rebellion among the other women."

Jan motioned the woman to the entrance of St. Lambert's Cathedral.

"What is your defense?" he said.

"Most Honorable King David, I have been taken against my will," the wife replied. "Our preachers have pledged that all women have a choice to whom they are wed for we are neither male nor female in Christ Jesus."

"Step forward woman," King Jan said.

He motioned to one of his guards who handed him a sword.

With one swift motion Jan swung the weapon against her neck and the wife's head bounced from her body. Landed on the steps.

Plop. Plop. Plop.

Blood spurted toward the sky.

"Wives obey your husbands as unto the Lord our God!" Jan commanded. "Let this be a lesson to all who would disobey. We will meet here at the same time tomorrow for another lesson on the duties of women."

The Amish Time Traveler

The next day King David called the city to watch him lop off another woman's head for taking two husbands. God ordained polygamy. The devil worked through polyandry.

Anna felt helpless.

She knew she had to go to Preacher's bed at his command.

She feared having a child... bringing a baby to the land of starvation.

She feared remaining childless... which necessitated Preacher's daily bedding.

But the constant terror gave way to apathy.

Hester and Clara helped her keep her senses.

Without them she would have thrown herself from the wall and to her death.

<< ☼ >>

One morning Hester and Anna split a turnip along with a robin Clara had managed to hit with her slingshot.

Anna felt as if she wanted to hit someone.

The turnip relieved the bite of pain but hunger still gnawed at her belly.

Fear gripped her body. If any of their neighbors sensed that the home of Bernard Rothman had food Anna and her sisters would be killed for it.

Guards banged on our door.

"Everyone out." They shouted. "By order of our king."

Anna felt half conscious. She pulled her body up off the chair and walked out the door. Hester and Clara each took one of her hands as if they knew they had to steady her.

The winter air reminded her that she'd left her shawl back in the kitchen but she didn't mind. The cold reminded her she still lived.

Preacher led them to stand behind King Jan and his wives in the front of the cathedral. Anna stared at his newest one – feeling as if she were transfixed by the girl's beauty. She remembered the rumors.

Build That Wall

How her neighbor had complained to the guards that she needed another blanket.

How Jan redeemed her from prison.

"These people are starving!" Jan's wife said.

"Hush," King Jan said. "They are a rebellious. Evil has entered their souls."

"They need food," she said. "You have a stable full of horses who eat well while these people starve."

"Have you still not learned to obey me?" he said. "We will ride our steeds in victory over the lawless heathen. None of the horses must be harmed. My subjects smell of disobedience. They must watch and learn from me."

Anna glanced at King Jan's face and remembered her last thought.

This wife will die too.

Chapter 13

Anna awoke in the bed she shared with Hester.
Clara sat beside them.
"Last night you fainted and we had to carry you to bed," Clara said.
"Preacher told the king you were pregnant and we were allowed to bring you home," Hester said.
"The king congratulated us all and Preacher smiled. I've never seen him smile before." Clara seemed proud of herself and the role she played.
Anna's whole body shuddered despite her effort to control it... What if Preacher was right?
Her heart sank.
Hester grabbed another blanket and tucked it around her. "You're shivering," she said. Then she lay down next to Anna and Clara took her place on the other side.
Anna thought of her baby. How would she feed it?
"You're suffocating me!" Anna screamed. "Go away!"
Her sisters tiptoed from the room and whispered behind the closed door.
But Anna didn't care.
For the first time in her life she wanted to die.
She remembered how she and Hester huddled in the ruins of their house next to their dead parents until they lost track of the days.
She remembered how she feared she'd lose her mind.
Only yesterday she'd walked next to a family.
One of the mothers fell to the ground dead
Her baby still attached to her breast.

Build That Wall

The father and sister-mother bent down to check on the starved woman then moved her out of the way. The furtive way they picked up the child convinced Anna they planned to eat it for dinner.

Anna did nothing.

She had no proof. Even if she could convince someone to do something she didn't have the energy to move.

Would her own baby be someone's food?

Woe is the day I was born... the day of my conception! She thought she remembered a verse like that from the Bible.

Then she remembered nothing.

<< ☼ >>

"Here. Put these on," Hester whispered. "Preacher's getting us out."

Anna forced her eyelids open and tried to move. She relaxed back in bed feeling as if she could sleep forever.

Hester manipulated Anna's shift over her head and pulled a pair of breeches up to her waist. Then she and Clara helped her to a chair where they added her shirt and jacket.

"I just want to sleep." Anna tried rise and crawl back under her covers.

"Stay here. Let Clara help you while I finish." Hester placed a bowl upside down on Anna's head and cut around the bottom – as if she were a boy.

The family gathered in the back yard.

"We have to slip out separately." Preacher patted Anna's belly.

"May the God of Abraham, Isaac and Jacob be with you," he said.

"Aren't you coming with us?" Clara said.

"Too risky. We'll meet up afterwards," he said. "Hester knows what to do."

Anna shook her head to clear the nightmare of animated cabbage heads who danced an eerie Halloween seduction scene. She reached out to touch one.

Poof.
They all disappeared.
A sharp pain cut through her stomach.
She crumbled to the ground.
"Here," Clara said. "Let me help you."
Soldiers called in the street. "The king demands your presence at the chastening."
"Lose yourselves in the crowd," Preacher said. "I'll meet you afterwards... by the river."
Anna and her sister wives shuffled to the square.
King David's eight wives lined on the top step of the cathedral.
King David – draped in embroidered silks with jeweled golden rings on each finger and a heavy crown on his head rode a regal white horse draped in purple tapestries. He led his steed up the steps and dismounted before his eight wives who bowed to him in respect.
"For the husband is the head of the wife even as Christ is the head of the church." He shouted to the starving crowd. "I shall show you an example of God's decree. No woman shall disobey her husband."
"Tell us woman!" he yelled to Peter Simons' second ex-wife. "You have disobeyed me three times! What is your defense?"
"I look across this group of people and see they are starving." She stood tall as if she felt secure in her righteousness.
"Deacons!" Jan said. "You know your duty."
Two Dutchmen held the woman's hands and led her to the chopping block where they forced her head down on top of it.
With a shout of rage King Jan threw his gold-hilted sword in an arc and his wife's head landed on the stones. Blood shot down the steps... across the crowd.
"Dance, my wives," he ordered. "For God's will is done."
"I will sing unto the Lord for he has triumphed gloriously," his first wife sang. She joined hands with her sisters.

Build That Wall

One deacon pulled a mouth harp from his pocket and played the tune. Another pumped his accordion... and the wives of Jan danced in unity.

Anna's stomach wretched but there seemed to be nothing left inside.

Other than the king's stable all the other animals had been eaten.

Along with the fish.

Gardens had been stripped months ago.

Anna wanted to go back home and sleep.

King David forbade hiding behind closed doors.

Maybe she could pull the covers over her head and sleep with the doors open.

<< ☼ >>

Hester led Anna and Clara to the river bed.

"Quiet. Don't make a scene," Preacher said. "Act normal."

"What's...?" Clara began.

"Quiet! Wife!" Preacher spoke in his soft voice that must be obeyed. "Jan's temper's satisfied for a bit. We must move now."

He looked at them with an expression of sadness.

"I'm sorry," he said. "I know the scripture but he's worse than Von Waldeck. Stay with God."

And he disappeared.

As if by magic.

Hester seemed unphased. "Follow me," she said. "He's made an arrangement with a farmer."

<< ☼ >>

"A bunch of rebels. You Anabaptists!" The man looked at the three girls. "You smell like death from miles away."

He shook his head as if he were disgusted.

"Children. Mere children you are... no older than my own youngsters," he said. "Guess you can't be blamed for it. Get yourselves in the wagon before y'all fall down from starving."

Anna studied the lumpy blankets for food.

The fields looked as if the army stripped them bare for as far as she could see.

"There's a cabbage. Hidden," the farmer said. "You'll have t' eat slow. I don't want y'all to throw it back up."

Anna dove in the wagon to search the covers.

Hester held her back. "Save your strength," she said. "Let me take care of you."

Anna leaned back on the side of the wagon and Clara snuggled next to her. Hester tucked blankets around them and handed them each one leaf of cabbage.

"Here," she said. "Eat. Slow!"

Anna's jaws hurt to chew. She felt as if she were too tired to move her mouth.

"Grind it into little bits!" Hester commanded.

Anna moved her teeth together. She'd never tasted anything better than that cabbage leaf. She let its juice trickle down her throat and felt hope for the first time since she'd left Preacher's bed.

"We're going south," Hester said.

"You bet we are!" the farmer said.

"We're supposed to be going north. Preacher said you'd take us to see Menno Simons!" Hester said.

"I've been paid well and I'll not shirk my duty. I'll get you away from this place but I won't be heading to death. That's for sure and certain," the farmer said. "Menno Simons seeks protection from a nasty man. Even the pope's men are afraid to enter his lands. Your man in Muenster may be stupid enough to risk your lives but I aint'. I'm taking you south t' safety. Not sure where yet but we're goin' south."

Anna finished her cabbage leaf.

Then leaned back to watch the scenery. It felt good to be outside the walls!

Build That Wall

They wouldn't starve today!
They had a whole cabbage to eat.
They passed a man and she looked up.
He looked as if he were skeleton.
His eyes seemed to have lost hope.
Then he fell in the ditch and didn't move.
Half a dozen people surrounded him snarling like dogs for a scanty piece of meat.
Anna felt ashamed.
She should care more.
She should want to stop this nightmare but exhaustion pulled her to the bed of the wagon.
The farmer urged his horse to pick up his pace.
South.
Always south.

A sign read Tauberbischofsheim.
They drove over the stone bridge and up the cobbled main street.
The farmer drove around to the back of a bakery and unsaddled his horse. "The women of the house need help with the spinning and tailoring. Your preacher said you learned that skill from your dead parents."
Hester nodded and stood. "Alexander's learned to spin real well. He was too young and skinny to help with the animals. Clarence bustles around helping us as he can. We'd be right glad to help any family of yours."
It took a moment for Anna to recognize her new name. Yes. Alexander.
And Clarence in place of Clara.
Anna – or Alexander as they called her on this trip – alighted from the wagon and stepped on the pavement before a large stone dwelling.
She hoped they could sleep in a house again for once.

The Amish Time Traveler

<< ☼ >>

The farmer woke them in the night.

"The prince-bishop's coming tomorrow," he said. "He'll send his troops to every house and check for outsiders."

Anna jumped up.

"Are we in a hurry?" said Clara.

"If he finds out we're Anabaptists he'll kill us," Hester said.

"Why?" Clara said.

"Orders from the Pope," Anna said. "He has to give us the opportunity to confess before we die."

"Don't piss on my boots and tell me it's raining," Clara said.

"You know me better than that, young'in." The farmer patted the child's head as if he were her father. "I never try to put one over on you. Your sister Hester's such an attractive thing. If the bishop doesn't kill her for heresy he'll accuse her of bewitching him and drown her for witchcraft."

"What do you want us to do?" Hester said.

"Gather your things and meet me in the stables," he said.

"Let's go," Clara jumped from her pallet and ran for the wagon.

"Shush," the farmer said. "Quiet. I don't want trouble either. We'll tell anyone who asks that Anna and Clara are my two sons and Heather is my new wife. We sold some cabbages in Frankfurt and we're on our way home. You are good girls. You must NEVER mention the Second Reich to ANYONE!"

<< ☼ >>

Anna gained enough weight to feel every bump in her pregnant body but walking took energy so she rode in the carriage anyway.

She lost sense of time when they stopped at the Austrian mountain pass. She knelt at the stream and drank fresh mountain water... then fell exhausted to sleep in the grass.

When she awoke the farmer had disappeared and a man sat in the grass watching her.

"My name's Samuel," he said. "You're dressed like a boy but your sister says you're really a girl in need of a husband."

"Are you a Papist?" Anna said.

"Of course. It's the law," he said.

"I'm with child," Anna said.

"She told me," he said, "and I'm in need of a wife. At least I know you can bear children."

"Where'd the farmer go?" she said.

"He bought the weaver's house for your sisters... then drove out of town. He seemed to be in a hurry." Samuel pulled a hunk of cheese and a small loaf of bread from his pouch and set them in front of her. "Eat," he said.

Anna dunked her face in the stream and cleaned her hands and arms, then took a delicate bite.

"Goat cheese," she said. "The best! Who made it?"

"My mam. Frau Arabelle. Tante Ara for short. That's what you'll call her until we marry. I sleep in the loft and my mother has the bed. We'll have to add a room for her before the baby comes. Our spinster died last spring so your sisters took over her house. Mam did some of the weaving but she's so far behind. We sure can use your sisters."

"Can I call your mam Oma Ara? She'll be a grandma soon." Anna touched her belly. "See. The baby moved. It must like you. You can touch it. We're almost married."

Anna wondered about this man.

He felt safe.

Familiar.

His kind brown eyes reminded her of Jesus.

She sighed.

Thank you God, her heart prayed. Thank you for saving my baby.

Samuel reached to feel the movement. His face broke into a smile. "Oma Ara," he said. "I'm sure and certain she'll love the name!"

The Amish Time Traveler

That fall before the baby came a traveling tinker sang the news from Muenster:

Muenster's bishop caught King Jan
Along with his two preachers
Cut off their heads, their arms and legs
And stuffed them into cages.

He raised their bodies to the sky
And hooked them to the steeple
A lesson for the heretics
From above St. Lambert's Cathedral.

Crows and Ravens picked their bones.
Soldiers seized their treasures.
All the world a lesson learned
For Papal rule eternal.

Clara would have gladly shot those crows for them to eat before they left.

After the tinker left Hester showed Anna the tract she'd bought that was written by Menno Simons himself.

Anna kept it under her pillow until Pauline's birth. Then she buried it under the hearth to show her daughters in case they ever decided to search out his pacifist followers.

Dear brothers and sisters in Christ,

God is love. His love surrounds us. His love is within us and he calls us to a life or holiness and truth.

We must turn our lives over to him and we MUST love all people. We must not lift up the sword as the Muensterites who tried to force the will of God.

Even if we are burned at the stake, if our families are beheaded for the name of God we must not hurt others. We must not fight.

Build That Wall

We MUST be faithful and true to our one and only God through Jesus Christ. We must not get caught up in pride or injustice.

Unlike the Godless idolaters and Popish drunken whoremongers we must cleanse ourselves from all sin and lift our lives to the will and to the hope of our Savior.

Turn your hearts from the ways of the world and set your eyes upon God that you may know and do his will.
In the name of our Lord and Savior Jesus Christ,
Brother Menno Simons

<< ☼ >>

After Mam finished her story Papa moved back to his own bed and Katie returned to Oma Ara's side of the house.

She laid back under her the feather mattress she shared with. During the night Oma Ara looked down from her dreams to watch Katie sleep.

She seemed cold and alone.

Oma Ara needed to rouse herself and light the fire.

But her body refused to move.

She had joined the ancestors.

Her spirit blended with the dreams of her son – Samuel. She watched him carry Katie to his own cottage and place the child in the loft next to her older sister Pauline.

Oma Ara tried to wake her daughter-in-law who'd always seemed weak from her near starvation before she'd arrived but Anna's spirit rose to join the spirit world with her.

<< ☼ >>

They buried Mam and Oma Ara in the cemetery by the Catholic Church. Pounded two wooden crosses in the ground to mark their graves.

After everyone else left the gravesite Katie fell to the bare earth above her grandmother's body and sobbed.

The Amish Time Traveler

She raised her head and stared at the statue of the virgin in the alcove under the church bell tower and tried to feel Oma's presence.

Nothing.

"Mary, mother of God, pray for me in this time of trouble."

Still nothing.

"God of the earth. Caretaker of all that lives and breathes."

The blessed virgin smiled.

Katie's heart felt as if it would split apart like a tree struck by lightning. The huge crash would rip her in half.

Heart wrenching cries escaped her mouth.

The sounds of a wounded animal.

"Oma. I need you. Pray for me in my hour of need."

The sun dropped in the west when she brushed the dirt from her skirts.

She crossed herself. "Thank you holy mother."

Who did she pray to? Oma? Mary? The Holy Spirit of God?

Did it matter?

She tucked loose strands of hair back in her braids and headed home to Pauline and Papa.

Chapter 14

The smell of cabbage and pork met her outside of their log cabin. Katie opened the door to see Aunt Hester standing in front of the fireplace. She held Oma's big wooden spoon over Oma's cooking pot.

Pauline stood next to her with a smile on her face. Her neat blonde braids fell down the clean shoulders of her house dress.

"This is your new mother," Papa said.

Katie slammed the door and stared at them.

What did Papa mean?

Katie's mom died.

How could Papa bring this woman into their house?

"Where are your manners, child?" Aunt Hester spoke in a sweet voice.

False.

Why else would Papa let that woman touch Oma's things?

No. No. No. Katie wanted to scream.

She clasped her lips to keep the words from escaping.

She couldn't breathe.

Their cozy log cottage felt as if it shrank like the dirt closing around Oma in her grave.

"The priest married us this afternoon," Papa said.

Katie looked at his eyes to find a twinkle like when he told a joke.

No. He told the truth.

"You will call me Mother." The dreadful woman spat the words at her.

Never. Not until the cottage fire turned to ice.

"Katherine." Papa spoke in his sternest voice. "Show respect."

Katie closed her eyes and turned to Hester the Horrible. She wished she'd undone her braids so her hair covered her face. She bowed her head in deference vowing to never let this woman see her pain. If Papa thought this self-important snob could replace her grandmother and her own mother.

Katie ran outside and slammed the door behind her.

She raced to her friend's house and looked through the window to see him sitting at the table with his father. Her stomach rumbled. It must be time to eat.

She waited until his eyes met her in the secret sibling language. He blinked twice and went back to his food.

Katie ran up the mountain past the village bake oven. Stone cottages bordered the side of the cobbled road.

She remembered when she was little.

"Careful little girl." Aunt Hester had grabbed Katie's arm. "Didn't your Oma teach you manners?"

Katie felt the fire flash from her eyes.

"No. It doesn't look like it. My sister may be too tired to teach you but I'm here to keep you in line. Good thing, too."

"Sorry Aunt Hester." Katie looked at her aunt's cottage. Nothing out of place.

This horrible woman might not even be human.

Preacher probably let Mam and Clara get away from Muenster so he never had to see Aunt Hester again.

Katie immediately felt guilty.

Her own mother had told her of the dangers they'd lived through. Besides, Katie knew better than to run past her aunt's place. If she just didn't get so preoccupied all the time.

The woman gave Katie a shake. "Don't ever break my flowers. Is that clear?"

Katie closed her eyes and nodded. The poor blooms marched in straight rows even through the window boxes. They might die from boredom. They must get exhausted from trying to be proper.

From then on it would never be Katie's fault if anything happened to her aunt's plants.

Mam's ugly sister better not kill Papa.

Build That Wall

Katie ran to the secret place where she met her friend. Tears clouded her eyes.

<< ☼ >>

She watched water tumble over the rocks as if she were in a trance.

"I came as soon as I could." Steffi touched her arm and sat next to her.

Two years earlier she had called him Thor but when he went to live with his father Paul everyone had to call him by his middle name.

Steffen.

After the first Christian martyr.

It caused less trouble with the Christian rulers.

Katie called him Steffi behind his father's back.

Tears streamed down her face. It took time for her to talk. "I'm going to hell. The priest said that I have to love everybody or go to hell. But even God shouldn't ask me to love Hester the Horrible."

What a good name!

It sounded proper.

Steffi picked a branch from the creek and began to whittle the way he did when he thought hard about what to say.

"I don't know what hell's like." He rubbed the sides of the wood to make it smooth. "But it can't be as bad as living with that stepmother of yours."

Katie smiled. "You heard?"

"I wanted to come right away but I thought she'd have you locked in the attic or something. I decided to wait until dark and help you escape."

Katie listened to water sputter and bubble over the rocks. She felt the pulse of the earth course through her body.

Steffi broke the silence. "Remember what the father said at the funeral."

"We die once. After that the judgment."

"I think we should forget about Hester the Horrible and give Oma Ara our own ceremony. Tonight's full moon."

Katie stood and started to walk. No words.

They followed the bed of the creek climbing upwards.

A lone wolf howled.

"Thank you." Katie spoke into the darkness. "That's the way I feel too."

The owl hooted. "You. You. You."

"Yes. Me. Me. Me. I'm alone without my mam and my oma."

Chapter 15
1985

Kay felt the trance lift...

"Cool," Autumn said. "Were you there? I didn't recognize you this time."

"I knew you. Arabelle or Oma Ara," Kay said. "I saw through the eyes of your mam, and then as your granddaughter."

"Sure," Autumn said. "That feels right." She slid down on the dirt and ran her hands along the ground covered in pine needles. "Did you feel it too? Our connection to the earth.

"It's amazing," Kay said. "I thought I'd never feel such a kinship with the land outside Holmes County but it happened at Eden Manor and now here."

"I know what you mean. It's eerie," Steve appeared at the bottom of a path in the trees, then sat beside Kay and Autumn on the bench inside the broken down ruins of the old cottage.

"Where've I seen that amulet before," he said.

"Oh my. We forgot to put it back in its case," Autumn said.

Kay grabbed the box and slapped the tree inside.

"We just want to get a night of sleep before she travels through time again," Autumn said. "It can be exhausting for her."

"But I've seen it before. I dreamed I held it in these mountains in a crystal cave. I want to hold it," Steve said.

"Tomorrow," Autumn said.

She held out her hand and Kay gave her the case.

"I always wondered about that dream, too. The one where the light danced through the crystals," Autumn said. "Now I know. And you MAY find out tomorrow, young man."

Autumn stood and faced Steve as if she wanted to emphasize that the subject was closed.

Kay pushed herself up from the green earth and felt dizzy from the time change.

"My grandfather had an old copy of the MARTYR'S MIRROR in German," she said. "When we read those stories my parents acted as if the Catholic Church would return to their habit of torturing us at any time... as if 400 years hadn't passed."

"It brings back memories, alright," Autumn said.

"I can't believe you two," Steve said. "Talking about martyrs. The evil Catholics."

"That's right," she said. "What were you doing while we were gone?"

"I keep having flashes... as if I've slept in one of the rooms in this place. Then I went for a walk... and suddenly I'm here. Like I lost time or something," Steve said. "I've always wanted to experience something like this but now I wonder. Is it real? Or am I caught in a dream?"

"What do you think?" Autumn said.

Kay watched the conflicted look on Steve's face. First certain. Then wondering... as if he were sure he'd been wrong. And finally a defeated undecided look.

"You don't have to answer," Kay said. "I felt the same way at first."

"No one can tell you what to think. You have to decide for yourself," Autumn said. "Answers may evolve or remain vague."

"You guys are something else." Steve shook his head as if to clear the confusion from it. "I wanted to take this trip. It feels right but.... Maybe I have to sleep on it. Can we meet back here in the morning?"

"Sure," Autumn said.

Kay watched him walk back toward the inn. He paused next to the garage in back.

Kay shuddered.

It seemed as if a huge man would step from the shadows and attack.

"It smells like spring all of a sudden," Autumn said. "The seasons must come late here?"

"I wondered the same thing." Kay looked around her. A cluster of forget-me-nots seemed to appear in the woods, then disappear again. "Maybe it's just more memories resurfacing."

"Why would I be seeing it? I died back then," Autumn said.

"But maybe your spirit hadn't left yet," Kay said.

"Can spirits smell spring?" Autumn said.

Kay inhaled the mountain air. "I don't know. But summer seems to have returned. And you're not dead now, are you?"

"It doesn't matter," Autumn said. "At least I know that I carried on a sacred spiritual tradition. You and I were as close to each other in our mountain life here as we were in Queen Anne's England."

"You'd think we'd get tired of each other." Kay smiled to let her cousin know she joked. They leaned forward and hugged each other.

"I'm so glad I have you, Cous," Kay said. "I fought your break from tradition for so long, but now I'm glad you're so unconventional. I don't know what I'd do without you."

"Feeling's mutual," Autumn said. "Without you I'd never have gone back to Queen Anne's England OR to 16th century Deutchland."

The sun seemed to lean to the west.

Kay's belly rumbled.

"Let's go eat," Autumn said.

<< ☼ >>

Kay laid back under her feather mattress and felt the cool mountain air tickle her face.

When she breathed in the smell of pine and earth it felt as comforting and alive as if she'd returned home from a long vacation.

She felt her body relax into the comfort of sleep.

<< ☼ >>

"Awake. You sleepy head," Autumn touched Kay's shoulder.

"Leave me alone." Kay swatted her away.

"But Steve's downstairs," Autumn said. "He says he wants to be with you to try your amulet. He needs to leave tomorrow and doesn't want you to dream the day away."

"He's right. I just dreamed that I met scary man who came out of the garage. Give me a minute to get the image out of my head." Katie heaved her body out of bed and started dressing.

"Tell him I'm awake," she said, "I'll be down in a few minutes and make sure the coffee urn's full."

Chapter 16
1556

Katie and Steffi entered the crystal cave under a high moon.

They made a small fire, then shook the dust from their animal skins and laid them on the ground. They lay next to each other and gazed at the stars.

When the moon reached the top of the sky they both fed the fire and took their places for the rite:

"I Katherine. Defender of the One True God do raise the royal sword of truth and commission you Theodoric Steffen. Holy warrior. Protector of the oak. And guardian of nature."

Katie touched her oak sword first on Steffi's right shoulder then his left. "We must prepare ourselves for life."

Katie brandished the weapon above her head... then laid it on the ground. She and Steffi removed their clothes and dressed in animal skins. They each took a sprig of dry pine... then knelt and laid their dry branches on the embers.

"All things come of thee Oh God and of Thine own have we given thee," Katie said.

"May we be good stewards of thy gifts," Steffi said.

The pine needles exploded.

Then the children rubbed ashes on each other's faces.

They each lowered an egg-shaped stone and sprig of dried herbs into the fire.

"We sacrifice these gifts in the name of the one true God of Zipporah, Deborah and all the prophets... the God of all nature." The two children recited the words together.

Katie took a sharp stone from the edge of the fire and cut a slit in each of her wrists. Steffi took the stone and did the same. Blood oozed into their hands.

They looked into each other's souls and joined hands and forearms over the fire. "May our blood mingle. May we be as one. Our hearts. Our souls. Our spirits. Now and forevermore."

A drop of blood fell into the fire and sizzled. A curl of smoke brought tears to Katie's eyes.

"May the bond we make today...," Katie said.

He finished her sentence. "Never be set aside."

"May I do my duty as a priestess."

"And I as priest. We will follow each other wherever we go."

"The trees." Katie looked to the bear face of the cliff. "The water and earth serve as our witnesses."

"And the animals our kin," Steffi said. A pair of hawks circled high above them.

Steffi took the amulet from his neck and placed it around hers. Seven crystals from the cavern adorned its branches – an heirloom from Oma Ara and her mother's mother's mother back as many generations as they could remember.

"May we eat from the tree of God's good and only knowledge. May we do what is right," he said. His gray-green gaze did not waver. A breeze tugged his dark hair away from his shoulders.

"We seal this oath with a kiss," they said in unison. A flutter rose from Katie's center. Surprise. She wanted to kiss him again. Longer.

He pulled away. Their fingers parted.

She blocked the pain from the crusting on her wrists. "We are one." The priestess performed the benediction.

"Nothing can separate us," said Priest Steffi.

"Blessed be."

Build That Wall

<<☼>>

They slept on the skins in the crystal cave until the sun created a rainbow around them.

Steffi's gray-green eyes seemed kind.

His cut brown hair lifted in the breeze.

They took turns feeding the fire.

Katie scattered salt, earth and herbs over the flames. The wind seemed to sing through her ruffled hair.

"Oma said I will hear your voice after my 12th birthday." She called to the sun.

"I am the voice of the spirit of God. The voice of knowing." She felt the voice in the depths of her belly. "Oma's spirit lives. Together you and she learn together in this life and the next."

"The Catholic priest said…."

"He promised everlasting life in heaven playing harps on streets of gold."

In a vision Katie sat on the shiny road playing a harp.

The five note melody filled her soul.

Forever?

BORING!

"I want to learn!" Katie screamed.

"Focus on LOVE." The wind whistled through the cave entrance. "The church message brings us to God. Its leaders make rules. They demand you to betray your own calling."

Katie lay on the ground and waited for the earth to come back into focus.

"You heard it too?" Steffi said.

"What did it tell you?" Katie said.

"To listen to the wind. To speak to each other and no one else about what we hear." He stretched out on the ground next to her.

"What about Papa and Pauline?"

"If Hester the Horrible thinks you can't talk…." He let the suggestion hang.

"She can't force me to tell her where we've been." Katie wondered why her father married her. She may have been Mam's sister but they had nothing in common.

"Hester the Horrible would get rid of us if she could," Steffi said. "She wants us to treat her as if she were our lord and master. She thinks we owe her penance for breathing the air she owns."

"That's the truth." Katie couldn't argue.

<< ☼ >>

When Katie returned to the cottage Hester the Horrible sat in Oma Ara's rocking chair next to the fire mending socks.

Papa set his wooden bowl full of soup on the table. "Where have you been, Pepper?" His eyes held a deep sadness that seemed to seep into his bones.

Katie ran and clung to him.

He hugged her as if he'd never let go. "Your mother and grandmother are gone. And your sister Pauline's been in the loft crying for the three whole days you were gone. She thought a wild animal ate you."

Katie called on every muscle in her body to keep the words inside. Hester the Horrible would twist every single one. Use it against her. Against Papa.

"She's too big…." Hester the Horrible said.

"Woman. Quiet." Papa never talked to anyone else like that but the woman deserved it.

The air in the cabin sparked lightening.

"Tell me Pepper." Papa smoothed Katie's hair back from her face. "Where have you been?"

Katie didn't move. The cabin never seemed so stuffy before Oma and Mam died.

"Do you want to go outside?"

Katie looked into his eyes. She hoped he could see the yearning in them.

Build That Wall

"Hester. Katie and I'll take a walk. Keep my supper warm and don't look for us."

<<☼>>

Katie gulped the fresh mountain air.
She remembered her talk with Steffi.
Would Papa keep secrets from his wife?
Too soon to know.
"We searched for you for two days but your tracks went into the creek. I began to think you drowned. Hester wants me to beat you for this."
They walked to the village crossroad in silence.
Turned down the cobbled road.
Dark shadows flitted past the blacksmith shop. Too late for the ping, ping, ping of the smithy Phillip's hammer.
In the lower meadow they sat on a log bench.
The owl hooted above them.
Katie stood in front of him. Pointed to her mouth and shook her head.
"You don't want to talk?" Papa said.
Katie moved her head back and forth. Then waited.
"I may have made a mistake. Marrying your Aunt Hester. But I need a wife and it's done," he said.
A marriage contract lasted for life. The village made certain of that.
Katie sat back down and leaned her head against his shoulder.
"I let your oma raise you and she did a good job. Now I'm jealous of all the time you had together."
Katie snuggled next to him.
Let him hold her close.
"Did something terrible happen to you these last three days? Did you lose your tongue? Is it Oma Ara's death?"
Katie didn't move.

The Amish Time Traveler

Big sobs shook Papa's body. Then his body grew still. He didn't speak until the moon stood tall in the sky and the night sounds quieted.

"I don't know how this happened. And you can't tell me," he said.

Katie let her body relax in his hug.

"I'll talk with Hester. Tomorrow she can say she's the long suffering step-mother to a poor deaf and dumb girl," he said.

Pity.

Katie didn't want Hester the Horrible's pity.

But the alternative?

The warning Katie's received in front of the crystal cave rang in her ears.

She squeezed Papa's hand.

"You can live in the room next door with your Aunt Clara if you'd like. Does that sound good?" he said.

She moved away from his shoulder and nodded her head up and down as fast as she could.

"I'll give you a whistle. You and Steffi or Pauline can take the sheep and goats to pasture. You'll get away from the village and roam the mountains you love."

Katie stopped her cry of joy and hugged him tight.

Papa laughed. "I almost envy you, Pepper. You might be the smartest one of us all."

<< ☼ >>

Hester the Horrible snored behind the curtains to the bed when Katie and her father slipped into the cabin. Katie climbed the ladder to the loft and fell asleep in her sister Pauline's arms. Tomorrow she'd climb over to the other side of the loft and climb down to Aunt Clara's side of the house.

Chapter 17

The rooster's crow cut through the crisp morning air.
Katie jumped out of bed.
Quiet. So she didn't wake Aunt Clara.
She opened the shutter a crack and looked out the window. Glancing at the clothes she'd set out for the day Katie took her every day dress off the hook next to the window and slipped it over her shift.
Fastening the front with one hand she slid down the ladder on Papa's side of the loft because Aunt Clara awoke at the slightest noise.
Soft snoring sounded behind Papa's bed curtains.
Katie tiptoed past the oak trestle table. She patted Pauline's wedding chest next to the door.
It was only made of wood but it seemed as special as if it were pure gold! Pauline filled it with everything she needed to take up housekeeping. After the wedding Philip would load it on a wagon and take it home with them.
Katie grabbed her shawl off the wall-hook and lifted the cottage door on its hinges in her own practiced way. She let herself out without a squeak.
She braced herself against the cool morning air.
She passed the gray form of the rooster pecking for his unseen breakfast and she looked back at her cabin.
The path appeared to shine even before the sun rose.
Hester the Horrible made her sweep it clean last night. She would make another list as soon as she woke up.
Busy work.
She never ran out of it.

<< ☼ >>

The Amish Time Traveler

Katie skipped on one foot, then the other until she came to the biggest building in the village.

It made her cottage seem small.

Insignificant.

Even though she couldn't read the sign under the bell tower she knew the words, "Holy Catholic Church of The Blessed Virgin."

She loved to watch the mother and child in the wall above the red door.

Today the Blessed Mother seemed extra kind.

Morning dew looked like tears on her cheeks.

Are you crying? Katie wondered.

Why would you cry on Pauline's wedding day?

Oh well. Katie turned to Oma's and Mam's grave markers and knelt down on one knee to cross herself. "In nomine Patri, et Fillii, et Spiritu Sanctum. Amen." She whispered.

Tears filled her eyes.

Still.

She missed her Oma Ara and Mam so much!

They had understood… sometimes without even talking.

Katie sighed and started back down the path.

"I'm twelve. Too old to cry." She spoke out loud… then looked around to make certain no one heard.

Good.

It seemed harder and harder to keep quiet.

One of these days…

Strains of an old hymn sang from the church organ.

At least one other person rose early.

The Latin words seemed impossible so Katie made up her own words.

Hester the Horrible would call it sacrilegious but even God couldn't be that strict!

"Love. Love. Spring is a time for love." Katie hummed her truth.

She hoped she wasn't awfully bad.

"Love. Love. Spring is a time for love." The organ rang out.

Build That Wall

A forget-me-not bloomed beside the road.

Katie picked it and touched it to her nose.

No smell. But pretty.

She examined the flower. Five blue petals attached to a white center with a green stem.

Perfect. The first one of spring. A good omen.

In a few days the trees would explode in bloom.

By then Pauline and Philip would be an old married couple.

If she and Steffi got to the secret patch of flowers on the mountain they'd be back before anyone else got out of bed.

Katie stopped and listened to the hush that comes before the birds scold the rising sun.

She inhaled the chilly air.

The sweet taste of new pine.

A mist rose through the gray valley and moved towards her.

She shivered... rubbed her hands on her shawl and planted her feet on the ground to look across the valley. The earth's cool pulse coursed through her veins.

Anything seemed possible on a perfect day like this.

Steffi's tavern stood on the right side of the T with a barn attached to its back.

Because Steffi's Papa was the richest man in the village he had a milk cow as well as a goat and some chickens.

Katie opened the top barn door.

"Steffi." She stuck her head inside and whispered. "Steffi, where are you?"

No one answered.

She closed the door and walked to the front of the tavern.

The cluster of houses sat on the narrow plateau called Ffernpass about a quarter of the way up the mountainside.

A few stone cottages hemmed the cobbled main road.

No front yards.

Katie looked up past Hester the Horrible's cottage.

Someone else lived there now.

The Amish Time Traveler

Down the mountain she saw the outline of Philip's barn where he worked as the blacksmith. The fields below his place appeared to be enveloped in fog.

Spring water wove down the mountain in a stream.

It gurgled under a bridge in the middle of the road and splashed down the other side seeming to cut the village in half.

Katie found no signs of Pauline's beloved flowers at its edges.

A strange dog pulled on its chain in Steffi's front yard. It raised its head and stared at her.

She walked closer but it rose on its haunches and released a mournful howl.

Goosebumps ran up Katie's arms.

Down her back.

Maybe Steffi had visitors. That's why he still slept.

Chapter 18

Katie walked back to the barn and looked inside.
Maybe Steffi….
Two large hands grabbed her. One twisted her arm up behind her. The other covered her mouth and pulled her into the dark.
Katie opened her mouth to scream.
"Hush!" the man snarled. "Stay quiet and you may live."
Terror shot through Katie's body.
She swallowed hard to keep her stomach in place.
The blood in her body seemed to turn to ice.
The rough hands pushed her into a corner of the stall.
She flailed uselessly against the man's strength. Her nose caught the edge of the feeding trough and thick gooey warmth oozed down her throat.
Wriggling one hand free she tried to wipe away the blood.
The man threw her against the wall. Again.
Took a chunk of hay and stuffed it in her mouth.
"I said be quiet." He growled.
She tried to scream but the air left her lungs.
If only she could sit up and cough!
Steffi would make the man stop!
Where was he?
No one would hear them through the thick stone walls.
Katie felt as if her brain filled with air and rose above her body until she watched herself from far away.
The man ripped open the front of his trousers and let himself down on her.
The air seemed to grow….
Puff her body bigger….
And tear her spirit away to a separate place.

The Amish Time Traveler

She saw everything....
And nothing....
Both at the same time.
A lightning bolt of pain united her two selves...
Forced its way between her legs and into her abdomen.

The storm of terror roared over her in waves seeming to swallow her body whole... as if she tossed like a leaf in its black funnel.

She seemed to be at its mercy forever....
Or for a moment that seemed like forever.
In a final gulp the storm flung her to the place of no breathing.

Katie looked down from the rafters at the strange young body that had been hers and tried to reattach herself to it.

"Konrad don't keep all the fun for yourself." A smaller man stepped in view.

"Never. Nothing beats a fresh young virgin." Konrad laughed patting him on the shoulder. Then he found a jug and took a swig.

"Konrad! What'd you do?" The second man seemed much younger. A boy. He sounded scared. "She's not breathing."

He picked up her comb and ran it through her hair as if it would make things better.

His hand touched the body and he pulled away dropping the comb in his pocket.

"Let's get out of here," Konrad said. "Calm down and grab your stuff. Walk slow so we don't look suspicious and we'll be gone before they start looking for us. Don't forget the jug."

Chapter 19

The world seemed alive.
Free as a dream.
Except for one thing.
Katie's body refused to move.
Blocking out everything else Katie focused on her breath.
She tried to blow the hay and blood from her mouth.
Nothing happened.
She centered her strength and tried to move the hands that weren't hers.
Then she moved her energy to make the feet move.
Nothing happened.
Feeling frantic she tried to make the body breathe and move at the same time.
A simple task such a short time earlier.
Still nothing.
"NOOO!" Katie's spirit moaned. "NOOOO!!! I'm not ready to diiiiiiie. I want my body back."
But her shell lay still... in the corner of the stall. Motionless.
Its brown eyes appeared glassy.
Long strawberry braids unraveled.
Blood caked across face and the once-straight nose that leaned to the side.
Time ceased.

<< ☼ >>

She sensed Steffi's presence.
She wanted to touch him.
Warn him.

The Amish Time Traveler

He whistled a low sweet tune... as if he were afraid to wake his papa.

Stepping from the gray dawn through the open barn door his thoughts clouded above him. "She must be here but she couldn't have been waiting long."

His body fell beside her.

Limp.

He pulled her torn clothing back in place and grabbed her to him. "Katie come back to me. I can't let you go. My little Pepper. My little Pepper."

He pulled her hand to his lips and kissed it. Then rubbed the small forget-me-not still in its grasp.

He rocked back and forth as if trying to keep her warm.

His brown hair appeared black.

His cherry cheeks seemed sunken and scarred.

His nose stood out from his face.

His gray green eyes grew dark.

He looked as weathered and windblown as a stranger.

"Steffi," her spirit exuded his name. "Steffi. I want to feel you next to me so we can pick flowers."

He couldn't hear her.

He clung to her lifeless frame as if he were lost to the sounds of the waking village.

"Get a move on." His father Paul walked through the door. "Sun's up and chores need doing."

Paul looked closer. "Jesus! Mary, Mother of God!" His voice came out hoarse and rose to a yell. "Boy! What've you done?"

"No! I found her like this. We're supposed to pick flowers for the wedding. But she won't move."

"Steffen," Paul fell to his knees and wrapped his arm around his son, then jumped up. "Those men. The ones who stayed here last night. They're gone!"

"I'll make them pay." Steffi laid Katie back on the hay with the gentleness of a grandmother.

"Yes we will," Paul said. "We will."

Build That Wall

"It's too late. And I'm still here." Katie tried to speak.

Paul ran to the door and grabbed the horn.

The one for emergencies.

Steffi pulled Katie's shawl from the hay and laid it across the body. Then he rubbed his sleeve across his face to erase any trace of emotion.

Grabbing his hunting horn from its hook he walked straight past his father toward the road.

"Good luck to you." Paul called to the retreating backside. "We're right after you. Soon as the women take the body."

Steffi rubbed his sleeve over the corner of his eye to erase the tear that escaped his rigid upbringing.

<< ☼ >>

At the T in front of the inn Steffi paused and looked both ways before walking down the mountain.

He'd make those fatherless sons pay for this.

If only he hadn't listening to their stories half the night he might have met her in time.

Protected her.

Now he'd settle for getting even.

He'd memorized every square inch of the countryside. It'd be easy to find sailors on leave.

<< ☼ >>

Katie's spirit sensed Steffi's presence leave when Hester the Horrible stepped through the door.

Her face appeared to be made of stone and her eyes stared straight ahead as if she were too tired and worn to show emotion.

Like all rugged mountain woman she took pride in preparing for anything life gave.

Grief wasted time.

Katie's spirit expected her body to sit up at the sight of her stepmother's stern presence.

She expected her body to apologize profusely for causing trouble on Pauline's wedding day.

But it didn't talk or even move.

Now Hester the Horrible would NEVER hear Katie's voice.

It should have been a happy fantasy but Clara's face appeared next. Ghost white.

Hester's face looked blank and tired.

Pauline shuffled behind them and sat on the hay without words.

Talk wasted energy. Besides, what could she say?

Hester knew what to do.

As soon as they straightened Katie's body and wrapped it in the shawl Papa carried the lifeless form in his arms as if she were a baby.

The three women followed him back to the shepherd's cottage in silence.

Chapter 20

Katie sensed her part in the portrait frozen in time.

Snowy nights sitting in front of the fire telling stories blended into the log cottage tucked in the side of the mountain.

The thatched roof and walls covered in mud stucco seemed untouched by the long winter.

Papa carved wood.

Katie and Pauline knitted sweaters.

Mama and Oma Ara spun yarn.

Last fall Katie helped Oma Ara card and spin the wool herself for a new dress.

They washed it in a vat of boiling water. Oma Ara bought indigo from the traveling merchant to add to the goldenrod for dying the cloth to a beautiful forest green.

Of course Oma Ara wove the fabric herself when Hester the Horrible took sick last winter.

Weaving was Oma Ara's job after Grandpa died and before Mama and the aunts came to the village.

All of those scenes blended into one portrait along with the ideas behind them.

<< ☼ >>

At the cottage Papa and Hester the Horrible carried the body to the large plank table.

Hester boiled water and washed the blood from the body.

Pauline brushed Katie's hair in long smooth strokes. Then she climbed to the loft and brought down the best dress Katie had ever owned.

After the two women prepared the body Pauline platted Katie's long strawberry braids and laid them straight on the soft green fabric.

Pauline stepped back. "She beautiful."

Katie wanted to touch her.

To thank her.

But she could only remain beside her old cold shell and try to recapture the portrait.

How precious her life had been!

She should have talked to those she loved.

Why had she cut herself off from Pauline and Papa?

Why had she hated the freckles scattered across her face?

"They look like pepper sprinkled on your nose. That's why I call you Pepper," Papa had said. By the way he looked at her she knew he thought she was charming.

Why had she always envied Pauline's blonde hair and clear skin?

How could she have hated anything about herself? She'd trade her very own body for anything.

If she could be alive right now she'd prefer red hair and freckles no matter what.

Katie's spirit noticed the little knob – the imperfect birth mark on her right ear three quarters of the way up from the bottom of her lobe.

When she lived it seemed like the only imperfection she and the nearly perfect Pauline shared.

Regrets came too late!

The portrait closed and the frame of death caged her final wishes.

Pauline hid her face on Katie's shoulder and clung to the body. Sobs wracked her form.

She pulled herself away and sat in the corner on a three legged stool looking dazed.

Hester laid two smooth round stones on Katie's eyes.

"NO!" Pauline grabbed them and ran outside to throw them high in the trees.

Build That Wall

The warm sun burst into the log home.

"Pauline. You come back here." Hester the Horrible used her sternest voice.

Katie wanted to hit her.

She knew Pauline went to her place along the brook by the meadow.

Katie stayed in the cottage to watch what happened next.

Chapter 21

The women from Ffernpass took turns filing through the cottage.

Alone.

Or in pairs.

Each person mirrored Hester's worn look.

Each spoke in short sentences with the same submission to inevitable tragedy.

Extra words wasted time.

"What an obedient girl."

"I'm sure you'll miss her."

"Such red hair."

"Must be God's will."

"Can't question Him."

"It's a test."

"First your mother-in-law and your sister. Now this."

"Let us know what we can do."

"She was such a tomboy."

"She was like my own daughter." Would the cottage collapse in one big heap at Hester's words?

Surely nature would not stand for the big fib!

The women continued as if nothing happened. "You still have Pauline. That's a comfort."

"Speaking of Pauline, where is she?"

"She just needed some time alone," Hester said. "I'm sure she'll be all right."

"I'm sure she will."

"She needs to face up to this thing. We all have tragedies."

"She'll be back soon enough."

"What a shame. Her wedding day and all."

"She'll marry tomorrow as well as today."

Build That Wall

"I'm sure she will."

When the woman finished giving their regards they helped Hester and Pauline prepare food for the wake.

Without a way to preserve the body it would be buried before sundown.

The next day was the Sabbath and the priest insisted that all work must be done before then.

<<☼>>

Pauline ran to the lower pasture where the stream grew wide and the animals came to drink.

She flung herself down on the damp grass.

Katie remembered what it felt like to lie on the earth and absorb its strength.

At sixteen Pauline was a woman.

Katie could never speak to Pauline ever again?

Since Pauline announced her engagement Katie had tried to be happy for her. But just imagine, cooking and cleaning every day!

Pauline didn't seem worried about it.

Was she trying to be brave?

Would a complete set of new linens, a goose down blanket and two pillows, a set of wooden dishes, two new dresses, an extra set of undergarments and a night dress embroidered in forget-me-nots be enough to make Pauline happy.

The wedding chest full of those treasures seemed precious.

But now...

Pauline seemed to want to marry the village blacksmith.

She seemed to love the new set of cooking pots Philip made for her wedding present.

Was she in love?

Or did she just want to take care of the horses?

No one in the village owned any horses.

They were too expensive to feed.

The Amish Time Traveler

But the Baron sent them to Philip from time to time so he could bring them back to health.

Pauline's world seemed far away.

And close.

Both at the same time.

Each idea came to Katie with a matching image.

The image came into focus and faded into the framed portrait.

Women and children stood around the cottage as a suffocating cloud of emptiness hung over them.

Hot.

Like a featherbed quilt in midsummer.

Then Katie's spirit noted the call from Steffi's horn.

<< ☼ >>

He guessed right.

The men's thoughts seemed written in the air above them.

They took turns gulping the home-brew in a clearing.

"Peter. Know where we are?" Konrad said.

The older boy shook his head. He turned to the younger one. "Andreas. How'd we get here? In the middle of the woods?"

"Seems like we were trying to get away from something." Andreas bent over the rocks and released the contents of his stomach. "I think we drank too much."

"We're up too early," Konrad said. "Time for our morning nap."

The dog flopped on the ground between them.

A raccoon spied the shiny comb in Andreas' pocked and sneaked up to grab it.

Andreas flinched in his sleep.

The dog barked and chased the raccoon up a tree.

Steffi followed the sound.

Then stepped away to blow the alarm.

The three drunks failed hear the horn or the village men who carried axes, ropes and other implements for weapons while forming a circle around them.

Katie's papa kicked Konrad's leg.

"Why does trouble always seem to follow me?" Konrad rolled over and opened his eyes.

He spied the rope and jumped to his feet. "Peter. Andreas wake up."

"Where are we?" Peter shook his head.

"You can't hold your liquor," Konrad said.

Andreas tried to roll over and go back to sleep.

Konrad gave him another kick. "Get up. Now!" He pulled Andreas' knapsack out from under his head.

"You drunken bums." Konrad kept his voice low as if he hoped the villagers couldn't hear. "Keep your mouths shut and let me do all the talking. You don't even know how we got here."

Konrad took turns looking them each in the eye to be sure he had their attention. "Do you understand?"

They both nodded.

Papa spoke first. "Where were you this morning?"

"Is there trouble?" Konrad held out his hand as if to shake it. "I'm Konrad. And my nephews, Peter and Andreas. Can we help you?"

His voice sounded compassionate.

Concerned.

What a con man!

Papa stepped back and held his hands stiff at his side.

Paul stepped forward between the two men. "We already met. You three came in late and didn't want to pay the full rate so I let you sleep in my barn."

"I remember." Konrad hated it when they all blacked out at once. The boys needed to quit drinking. Paul's voice sounded as if they'd be blamed for something awful.

"You're not here alone." Konrad spoke in a pleasant voice. "It looks like you're searching for somebody. Can we help?"

"My daughter's been murdered." Papa snarled as if he wanted to grab Konrad on sight but... he needed to make sure he had the right man.

"You were in the barn where she was murdered last night," Paul said.

Konrad's face took on an immediate look of horror. "You've got to be joking!"

"That's Katie's!" Steffi grabbed for the comb sticking out of Andreas's shirt pocket.

Pushing Andreas out of Steffi's way Konrad beat him to it and held it in front of him. "How'd you get this? I've had so much trouble with you two. I can't leave you alone for one minute!"

He turned to Paul. "The boys were orphaned several years back. I've tried so hard to keep them out of trouble but this is the last straw! It'd serve them right if you strung them up."

"But you..." Peter whimpered. Konrad couldn't mean what he said. He always got them out of trouble.

On the other hand, he might be telling the truth. Maybe Peter had killed the girl and deserved to be hanged! If he could only remember.

"After all I've done for you... you have the nerve to talk back to me," Konrad said.

"But you were the one..." Andreas made his feeble attempt...

"I was the one who what?" Konrad said. "I was the one who took you in. I was the one who took care of you."

The men's thoughts hung above them and Katie saw how Konrad seemed impressed by his own words

He'd convinced himself that he spoke the truth.

In fact, he sounded too right to be wrong.

Andreas wondered how he could be guilty of such a crime. Maybe he deserved to hang!

"Come on boys. You're coming with us." Paul and Papa each grabbed one of youngsters. Held their hands behind their backs.

Katie's spirit watched Steffi's thoughts.

He worried about Konrad... as if he knew something seemed wrong. Peter and Andreas seemed too young... too innocent.

But his father and Samuel must be right...

Build That Wall

Steffi stood back while they dragged the boys to the sprawling oak tree.

The women left Papa's cottage and gathered to watch the men sling ropes around the branches.

The villagers' stony expressions relaxed.

"Thought you could get away with it!" Hester the Horrible screamed.

"Not in this village," someone else joined in.

Katie's spirit blocked out the rest of the voices

"I'm so sorry! I'm so sorry." Tears ran down Peter's face.

"God forgive us. Please forgive me." Andreas moaned.

The crowd fell quiet for the priest to say the last rites.

Then the agonized cries of repentance were gagged and the two bodies hung from two separate branches of separate trees.

Limp and motionless.

Swinging back and forth.

Dull eyes bulged from blood-filled heads.

The boys stared straight ahead. Seeing nothing.

As soon as they left their bodies and saw Katie's spirit they understood.

Katie watched them turn into bursts of light. Float toward the mountain and disappear.

Chapter 22

Pauline returned to the cottage yard and sat apart from the others on a bench with Philip. Her face frozen. Every so often he reached over and patted her hand.

The rest of the villagers appeared to be relieved when they walked back to the cottage... as if they were invigorated by the swift revenge.

A few wiped a tear from an eye.

Most had the same expressionless look that Steffi wiped onto his face before he left the barn.

No one cried.

The voices of the neighbors sounded as hollow as if they spoke of a stranger.

Did they lie when they called her a good girl?

Would they miss her like they said?

Samuel wasn't good with rules.

Every so often a stray tear escaped down one of his cheeks.

Hester the Horrible looked embarrassed by him but even in death Katie loved Papa for being true to her.

His kindness seemed to wash the framed portrait clean.

<< ☼ >>

"The wedding is postponed until after a suitable mourning period." The sun stood tall for the priest's announcement. "Rites for the dead will be said before sundown."

Papa, Steffi and Paul wrapped Katie's lifeless body in a blanket and carried her from the cottage down the short path to the church cemetery.

Build That Wall

Katie watched them lower her body into the hole beside Oma Ara's burial plot.

"In nomine Patri, et Fillii, et Spiritu Sanctum. Amen."

The shortest ceremony in history.

A plain white cross marked the head of the grave under the watchful eyes of the statue of the Holy Mother.

One drop of water traveled down the Virgin's cheek.

Chapter 23

The women brought out food they'd prepared for Pauline's wedding and the priest said the blessing.

"I bet you've never even seen a ship!" Steffi said.

"Christopher Columbus was a personal friend of mine. He said that the New World is more fantastic than you could ever imagine. The stream beds are pure gold," Konrad said.

Katie read the words above him and saw how he convinced himself of his own lies.

Again.

"Can't be!" Steffi swallowed the cold hard feeling he had in Konrad's presence.

"Trust me. It's more exciting than you can imagine." Konrad shifted his eyes toward the building behind Steffi so he wouldn't have to meet Steffi's eyes.

"The ships are bigger than your entire church building." He paused to heighten the effect of his words. "And the sails reach twice the height of the steeple." He seemed unsure whether or not he exaggerated until the words came from his mouth.

Katie saw his thought... these ignorant farmers believed anything.

"The wind catches the sails and carries the ship faster than a horse can run," he said.

The villagers listened... unsure whether he told the truth.

"I met Magellan before he tried to sail around the world," Konrad said. "I warned him that it was too dangerous. But he didn't care."

Well, his grandfather had seen the man from a distance.

That seemed to be the same thing.

Build That Wall

"If you love sailing so much," Paul said, "what are you doing around here?"

"I came back to the slate regions south of Muenster to settle my family estate and we're on our way back to Spain. I wanted to see the Mountains. I like seeing new places." Besides... it was safer that way.

He didn't want to run into certain people.

He hung his head and lowered his eyes. "Now that my family's gone I wanted to set Peter and Andreas on the straight and narrow. It's so sad. You try help others and you never know what will happen."

"Muenster. Have they recovered from the Second Reich?" Samuel said.

Katie's spirit saw the grey clouds of disgust rise from her father's words.

"It was God's kingdom on earth," Conrad said. "If Von Waldeck hadn't killed the leaders..." Conrad shook his head as if he were disappointed.

"A Northern Anabaptist named Menno Simons writes that Jesus taught peace. We should shape our swords into plow sheers," Samuel said. "What do you think of that?"

"Jesus also said that we'll all have wars." Conrad spat on the ground as if he were disgusted with the idea. "We protect our families. The Catholic Church has always slaughtered heretics. Now the Anabaptists do the same. Pacifism is naiveté."

Katie watched the red blob of pride hover above Conrad.

"How do you like that, Samuel?" he said. "Naiveté. A French word that means simple... unlearned."

"The Catholic Church is God's only church." Paul interrupted as if he were trying to stop a fight. "The Anabaptists do more than just break the law. Baptism is a sign of citizenship which they openly flaunt. When their children die before they receive the sacrament they go straight to hell. The priest baptized my boy on the day of his birth. I'd never risk sending him to hell."

Paul patted his son's back... but Steffi didn't seem to notice. He had a far-off look in his eyes.

"You said you're headed for a ship," Steffi said.

"I'm going to be a missionary to America... baptize the adult heathens." Konrad lowered his eyes as if he was ready to pray.

The men glanced around to see where the priest was.

Didn't Konrad know the dangers of talking like that?

"Luther was right. The Pope has no right to collect our money for himself. We don't need the Catholic Church to be Christians. But Luther didn't go far enough. The pope can't tell us how to pray and they can't MAKE us get baptized. It's a personal decision. For adults. Christ will soon come back to save his church and none of us want to be caught unready."

Konrad didn't live in Austria.

He was going off on a ship.

"Tell me more about sailing," Paul said. If someone didn't change the subject they could all be hung for listening to this heresy.

"Like I said...," Konrad began. "Luther's getting as bad as the pope... instituting taxes on the poor... turning his back on the needy..."

Steffi's eyes grew darker and his face grew harder.

Something felt wrong but he couldn't put it into words.

Katie tried to touch him.

To scream that the guilty one got away.

But nothing worked like it had.

How long would her sister postpone her wedding?

Would it matter?

Why stay aware when she was helpless to do anything?

Katie's spirit wearied of her lack of power.

She needed to warn Steffi...

But she found it impossible.

Maybe it didn't matter.

Even if Steffi knew... What could she do?

She might just as well rest.

Build That Wall

All of her sensations disappeared into a portrait of the life that had been Katie.

The frame melted into a white light... followed the dancing breezes up through the tall pines to the sky above.

<< ☼ >>

If she had stayed longer she would have watched Steffi walk straight to his room and wrap a few belongings in his extra shirt.

He tied them together on the end of a stick.

Grabbed his bow and arrows.

And walked down the mountain without looking back.

He was headed west to find the sea.

It would wash away the pain that clung to his soul.

Or maybe he'd travel to the gold-lined streams Konrad mentioned.

A world of wealth waited for him.

No one noticed him leave.

They were too busy listening to Konrad's stories.

Chapter 24

Kay opened her eyes to see Steve sitting next to her on the picnic blanket.

"Wow," he said. "That was SO COOL! My name was Thor, then Steffi. I lived here in a past life! I'm pumped! Let's take that walk in the woods we talked about back in the 16th century!"

He jumped up and pulled Kay by the hand.

"But Katie died!" Kay said. "How can you be so pumped?"

"What do you mean?" he said. "She and Steffi were just getting ready for her sister's wedding.

"Is that all you remember?" she said. He must not have come back to this life when she did.

"It was great! We celebrated solstice by the crystal cave," he said. "I can hardly believe it. Then we were going to the mountain to pick flowers. Let's go!"

"Give me a minute," Kay said.

Finally.

After meeting each other to observe three lifetimes they were going to reconnect with their memories.

Kay sighed in relief.

<< ☼ >>

Kay felt as if the same gravity that straightened the tall pines pulled them to a clearing on the mountain.

Steve moved a log over for them to sit on and eat lunch.

A breeze whispered through the trees.

Pine needles seemed to play a song. "Love. Love. Now is a time for love."

"Love. Love. Now is a time for love," echoed the sun.

He held her hand...
They gazed at the village below...
Let it speak to them.
He slipped his arm across her shoulder. She leaned closer and lay her arm across his waist for some time.

"Doesn't that church look quaint from up here?" she said.

"If it could only talk," he said. "It's been through two world wars. Plus weddings. Funerals."

"The statue of Mary looks as if she stands guard over the village cemetery." Kay let her eyes travel to the small clearing at the bottom of the village where the grass seemed especially green.

Plants of forget-me-not stood in front of wild daisies.

She stared at two ancient oak trees.

An involuntary shudder shook her body.

"My God!" Steve whispered. "Gallows. When did I see them before?"

Chills ran through her spine.

"I know I have," Kay said. She wondered why he'd returned to this century before she did – why he hadn't stayed for the end of Katie's life.

"No. I mean it. I've really seen them," he said. "They're so vivid it's haunting. Those trees have even more stories than the church."

Maybe he didn't want to handle anything bad. He only wanted good things... Kay squashed the thought.

"Just think. Secret trysts. Fights. Animals wandering off," he said.

She relaxed...
Let herself merge with their natural closeness.
She felt as if the two of them had always been –
This moment was all that mattered.

"Those trees were gallows for murderers... thieves," he said.

"I'm sure of it," she said. Even though he didn't stay in the 1500's he knew...

She remembered her seeing... before she traveled through time.

"Immediate revenge," he said.

"But the real criminal got away," she said.
"They buried the victim's body next to the church."
"In nomine Patri, et Fillii, et Spiritu Sanctum..."
"Amen."
"Amen."
They sat in the quiet.
Kay marveled in this connection....
Its centuries- old wonder.
He ran his hand through her strawberry hair.
Looked in her eyes.
"I care about you so much," he said. "I don't know how I let you come to mean so much to me in such a short time but I am madly uncontrollably in love with you like I have never been in love before."
Her whole being cried out to him.
Time lost meaning.
She felt as if an unknown force beyond them both pulled her straight into his soul.
She couldn't fight it...
Wouldn't if she could.
She closed her eyes and gave in.
Their lips touched in a gentle caress.
Soft.
Warm.
As if they both tasted well-aged wine.
She savored every drop.
"Love. Love. Now is a time for love," whispered the long-forgotten child named Pepper inside Kay's soul.
Kay took a deep breath.
The flowers. Pines.
Smells of spring soothed her.
"How could I ever forget my Steffi?" she sighed.

Chapter 25

    The damp mountain air wafted across the featherbed cover... tickled her cheeks. She snuggled deeper into her covers... relishing the comfortable womb-like feeling.
    "You're awake." Autumn pulled back Kay's quilt.
    "Don't do that!" Kay tried to snuggle in the warmth.
    "You and Steve were gone for an entire day! Do you think I can let you get away with sleeping when you have so much to tell me?" She sat on Kay's bed and bounced a bit as if to keep Kay's attention.
    "Only a day?" Kay said. "It seemed like years!" Her head felt as if she were swimming under water.
    "Did Steve come back with you?" Autumn said.
    "Of course. We took a walk up the mountain when we came back. It was Beautiful. We made love..." Kay sighed. She'd never felt so connected to anyone in her life.
    "He left you a note at the desk." Autumn handed Kay the envelope.

Dear Kay,

    Thank you for helping me take the trip back in time. I will owe you a debt of gratitude for the rest of my life.

    You helped me understand why I have always loved the sea. You have given me the ability to stand up to my parents and make a decision. I must find a life in sailing. I don't know where that life will take me, but I need to explore all of the oceans of the world.

    I'm sure you'll understand why I called a taxi and left early this morning to start my new adventure. I hope you and Autumn have a nice trip home.
Yours,
Steve

    Kay felt the tears run down her face.

"We made no promises," she said, "but…"

"Damn it. That's two lifetimes he's left me." She threw back her covers and landed with her feet on the floor. "No! Three… The bastard."

"I shouldn't have given you the letter… What happened to you after I left you in the 16th century," Autumn said.

"Don't you get it?" Kay stamped her foot. Sat back on the bed. "I've let Steve do it again. I gave everything and he walked out on me again. This is the third lifetime!"

"Did he walk out on you in the 16th century?" Autumn said.

"Well. It seemed like it," Kay said. "Konrad murdered Katie and Steffi left after the burial but he didn't stay for the rests of the funeral."

"And in England he had to escape the queen," Autumn said.

"This lifetime we could have finally spend time together and he left!" Kay let herself collapse in her cousin's arms.

Emotions.

Both the Katie from Austria and the one from Holmes County had blinked the tears back inside.

Kay would let herself cry.

Then she'd get back to her life.

Maybe Steve did her a favor.

He was too young and entitled anyway.

Chapter 26
Quakertown 1985

"So you had sex with Steve," Levi said.

The sun sneaked its light through the windows of Kay's row house... and Kay watched Levi's shoulders slump in sorrow.

No wonder!

She'd chosen another creep instead of his steady calm and dependable self.

"I'm an idiot when it comes to love," Kay said. "I sneaked away from the Amish – I know that's how most of us leave – but it doesn't make it right. Then after my husband raped me I just left... and trusted another man without substance... when all along you would have been there for me. You're an upright man of character... you lack the shallow selfishness of the men I chose."

"You said you didn't have anyone special in your life. What about Steve?" Levi said.

"I never saw him again. Like I said, I fall in love with the men who love themselves so much they don't have room for me." Kay wondered what was wrong with her.

Did she have a damaged heart that made her pick unavailable men on purpose?

Or did she have some other disorder?

Could she be autistic like so many of the Amish?

"I believe it's God's will. I'll marry you and raise the child as my own. My wife and I were not blessed with our own. " Levi's face took on the look of a man who made up his mind. He'd stay true to his decision.

An Amish man's word was his bond.

"Maybe it was a blessing," he said. "So many of the Amish these days have auto-immune disorders, dwarfism and grave birth defects.

Levi would never question her past again... just the way no member of the Amish church would question a person's behavior before they joined the church.

"I have twins," Kay said.

"Grandma B told me you're pregnant," Levi said.

"I am?" Kay felt as if she'd fall off her chair.

"She guessed you're several months along and she'd hate to see that ex of yours raising another child. She told me to decide what I want to do about it," Levi said. "I decided I'm glad. My wife and I couldn't have children but if you allow me to have another chance..."

He looked into her eyes.

She read yearning. Hope. Desire.

"Grandma B said I'm several months along?" Kay said.

Levi nodded his head. He looked way too serious.

"I hope she's a red-head who looks like you," he said.

"Grandma B's never wrong." Kay tried to think of a way out of this dilemma.

"Conrad." Kay threw her head on the table and sobbed. "After the funeral. The last time we had sex I said NO. He didn't listen."

Now she'd live with the constant reminder of her rape. Would her child disappear from her the way she left her own mother? Could she make another rash decision... run to a man again?

"I can't marry you just for the sake of a child," Kay said.

"Don't you care about me a little bit?" Levi said.

"I respect you enough to let you know what you're getting yourself into," Kay said. "How can you know what you want? Besides, I'm a time-traveler. You don't want a wife who leaves you home with the children while she goes off traveling through time. Do you?"

"God put the perfect mate in my life and I accept her however she comes to me. If you've traveled back to the time of Menno Simons then it is God's will. How can I question God's will?" he said.

"Does God have balls and penis?" Kay said.

Build That Wall

"Good point." Levi held out his hand and rubbed Kay's arm. "I understand how you think I should have said God's will instead of using the word his. We ARE talking about a spiritual being instead of a human but the Amish always refer to God as he and I hope you can accept that I change slowly."

"I see the professors at Eastern Mennonite College did their job," Kay said. "I like that you're able to learn. Do you have any faults?"

"I'm one of the most stubborn men I know," he said.

"Of course. You're Amish born. I'd expect nothing less! But I tell Annie and Andy they're focused. That adjective has a better connotation."

"I'm willing to take care of the children while you and Autumn travel if that's what you want. I think God knew I wouldn't have made the right mate for you back when you turned 16. I never would have had a chance to meet your twins."

"I'm hardheaded too," Kay said. "Maybe even more than you are."

"I'm counting on it."

"I'm thinking of becoming a Quaker."

"I'm 42 years old. Some of the boys I grew up with have a dozen grandchildren. My business pretty much runs itself. We don't need to have the traditional marriage as long as you don't go running off with guys like Steve."

"Are you going to let me forget about him?" Maybe she was wrong about his forgiveness.

"Of course. Do you plan on having more lovers?"

"I never planned on having any. I wasn't married anymore, if that makes a difference. And the baby's Conrad's."

"I figured as much. I've heard that children born after a rape are often larger, feistier. We may have a challenge on our hands," Levi said. He smiled as if he anticipated the task.

"My mind won't slow down," Kay said.

The Amish Time Traveler

"Are you saying? Of course. That makes sense. Your family always treated you different. Blame the victim bullshit. Do you think you are a child of rape?" His face flushed bright red.

Kay stared at him. She'd never heard him use a foul word in her life.

"When I think of the way your family…." He stopped, as if he couldn't continue.

"You guys did a number on Conrad though! He thought he'd just show up and the dumb pacifists would just give him their children." Kay smiled. Stood up to start a pot of coffee.

"And about time someone showed him up," Levi said.

"If we marry I'd finally make my family proud," Kay said. She wondered if she'd ever get over wanting her mother's praise… her sisters' admiration.

"It's been a long night. I'll have a lot to think about." She turned off the coffeepot. "I care about you deeply Levi. But I can't make a decision after no sleep. I can't believe I'm pregnant. I thought I had my cycle after Conrad. I must have been wrong."

"Go get some rest. I'll sleep on the couch in case the twins wake up before you do," Levi said.

"You can shower here if you want." Kay walked up the stairs to her bedroom.

How did one make a well thought-out decision?

She felt as if she were crazy. She'd do anything to protect her children.

She'd gained a new respect for Menno Simons.

With the recent airplane hijackings brought home the fact that the world was a dangerous place but the Amish, the Mennonites and the Quakers all refused to fight violence with violence. They chose peace instead. Both through prayer or meditation and through sustainable actions.

It seemed as if Levi had mellowed.

What did her gut say?

She stretched her joints.

Maybe things would seem clear in the morning.

Build That Wall

THE END

The Amish Time Traveler

RECIPES

German Chocolate Sauerkraut Cake

Preheat oven to 350 degrees.

Sift together:
1/2 cup unsweetened cocoa
2 1/4 cups sifted all-purpose flour
1 teaspoon baking powder
1 teaspoon baking soda
1/4 teaspoon salt

Rinse and drain 2/3 cup finely chopped sauerkraut. Do not squeeze dry. Add 1 cup room temperature warm.

Cream together:
2/3 cup soft butter
1 1/2 cups refined sugar

When they turn a lighter color beat in:
3 eggs, one at a time, beating between each addition
Add 1 teaspoon vanilla

To the creamed mixture, fold in 1/3 of the sauerkraut-water mixture alternating with 1/3 of the flour mixture. Do not overbeat.

Pour the batter into 8" floured pans fitted with waxed paper liner. Bake for 30 min.
Or use 9x13 pan and bake for 40 min. or until toothpick inserted near center comes out clean.

Can be frosted with

Cream Cheese and Peanut Butter frosting

    8 ounce softened cream cheese
    1/2 cup peanut butter (chunky or smooth)
    1 t.
    3 cups powdered sugar
    2 T. milk

Beat cream cheese and peanut butter until smooth.
Add powdered sugar 1 cup at a time.
Alternate with vanilla and milk beating to right consistency.
Spread on cooled cake.

Funny Cake

You will need pastry for one pie.
Preheat oven to 375°.

Cake mixture:
2/3 c. brown sugar
1/3 c. lard or butter
1 egg slightly beaten
½ c. milk or cream
1 t. baking powder
1 c. flour
1/2 t. vanilla

Bottom part.
½ c. white sugar
¼ c. cocoa
1/3 c. HOT water
¼ t. vanilla

For top part: Cream together sugar and shortening. Beat in egg. Add milk and vanilla alternatively with dry ingredients. Stir and set aside.

For bottom part:
Combine sugar and cocoa. Add hot water and then vanilla.
Pour bottom part into an unbaked pie crust. Then pour top part over it. Bake for approx. 40 min.

Ground Cherry Pie

You will need 1 – 2 pie crusts
Preheat oven to 375°.

Wash 2 ½ c. ripe ground cherries and place in unbaked pie shell. Mix ½ c. brown sugar and 1 T. flour. Dust over top. Sprinkle with 2 T water.

Crumbs (optional):

Mix 1 c. flour with 1 c. sugar. Press ¼ c. butter into the dry ingredients with a fork. Spread over pie for a topping.

An upper crust may be used instead of the crumbs.

Bake for 40-45 min.

Tapioca Pudding

4 c. milk
3 egg yolks slightly beaten
¼ c. minute tapioca
½ c. sugar
½ t. salt
1 ½ t. vanilla
3 egg whites beaten stiff

Combine milk and egg yolks in a saucepan. Add tapioca, sugar and salt. Let sit for 5 minutes. Bring to a boil stirring constantly. Remove the mixture from heat. Add vanilla.

Add 1/3 of beaten egg whites in a large bowl. Fold in tapioca mixture, then the rest of the egg whites leaving little pillows. Chill.

Garnish with whipped cream, tart jelly, or chocolate chips.

Graham Cracker Pudding

Crush together 1 pkg. graham crackers with 1 T brown sugar. Mix with 2 T melted butter.
Set aside for later.

You will need
　　½ c butter
　　1 c brown sugar
　　1 ½ c milk
　　3 T cornstarch
　　½ c. white sugar
　　2 egg yolks
　　1 c. milk

Simmer butter and brown sugar until browned a little. Add 1 ½ c milk and cook. Combine cornstarch, sugar, egg yolks, and milk. Slowly add to cooking mixture and stir until thick.

Place layer of cracker mixture in bowl. Add pudding. Then another layer and pudding.
　　Topping:
　　1/3 c. heavy cream
　　1/3 c. sugar
　　1/8 t. salt
　　1 t vanilla
　　Whip cream. Add other ingredients. Fold ½ into pudding. Reserve the rest for garnish.
　　For variation, add 2 sliced bananas.

Whoopee Pies

Preheat oven to 400 degrees.

1 ½ c. butter
3 c. sugar
3 medium eggs plus 2 egg yolks separated
Reserve the egg whites for filling.
2 t. vanilla
4 c. flour
1 ½ c. cocoa
2 ½ t. soda
1 t. salt
2 ½ c. hot water, need not be boiling.

Cream butter and sugar together. Beat in eggs and vanilla. Add dry ingredients. Gradually pour in water. Mix. Drop by spoon onto cookie sheet.
Bake for 10 to 15 minutes. Cool.

Filling:
1 egg whites
4 T flour
4 T milk
2 t. vanilla
1 ½ c. shortening
4 c. powdered sugar
Mix ingredients. Beat thoroughly.
Spread filling on bottom of one cake.
Sandwich with another cake.

Grandma B's Oatmeal Coconut Cookies

Preheat oven to 350°.
1 c. white sugar
1 c. brown sugar
1 c. lard
2 eggs
1 t. vanilla
2 c. flour
1 t. baking powder
1 t. baking soda
1 t. salt
2 ½ c. oatmeal
2 c. shredded coconut
Optional: ½ c. nuts.
For variety a small package of chocolate chips may be used instead of coconut.

Cream sugar and shortening.
Add eggs and vanilla, then dry ingredients.
Spoon onto cookie sheets.
Bake for 10 to 12 minutes.

Note: Lard makes a flatter cookie with a crisp taste.

Chow Chow

4 tart apples
4 c. chopped celery
4 c. chopped carrots
4 large sweet peppers with variety of color
1 c. sugar
2 c. vinegar
1 t. celery seed

Chop apples.
Cook chopped celery and carrots in a small amount of water until almost tender.
Add chopped peppers and apples.
Pour in sugar, vinegar and celery seed.
Bring to a boil.
Pack in sterile hot jars and seal.

Three Bean Salad

1 pound fresh, frozen or canned cut green beans
1 pound fresh, frozen or canned cut wax beans
1 15 oz. can dark red kidney beans
½ c. chopped red or green bell pepper
½ c. sugar
2/3 c. cider vinegar
1/3 c. canola, vegetable or olive oil
1 t. salt
¼ t. pepper

Drain beans.
Combine with pepper.
Toss with sugar, vinegar and oil.
Add salt and pepper.
Cover and chill overnight. Serve.

End of the Garden Pickles

 2 c. cucumber slices
 2 c. chopped bell pepper, any color
 2 c. chopped red or green cabbage
 2 c. chopped green tomatoes
 2 c. cut green beans
 2 c. diced carrots
 2 c. chopped celery
 1 c. chopped onion
 2 T celery seed
 2 T mustard seed
 4 c. apple cider vinegar
 3 c. sugar
 2 T turmeric

Soak cucumbers, cabbage, tomatoes and peppers in salt water over night using ½ c. salt to ½ gal. water.

 Next day:
 Cook beans, carrots and celery until tender, but not soft.
 Drain soaked vegetables and cooked vegetables.
 Combine vinegar, sugar and spices.
 Heat to boiling.
 Add all of the vegetables and simmer 10 minutes.
 Pack into sterile, hot jars and seal.

Green Tomato Pickles

1 gallon sliced green tomatoes
1 quart apple cider vinegar
2 cups dark brown sugar or raw sugar
1 T. whole or chopped cloves
4 sticks or 3 T. cinnamon
3 T. Redmond's Sea Salt

Cook tomatoes in water until tender, not soft. Drain.

In a separate pan combine vinegar, sugar and spices and heat to a slow boil for 15 minutes, then pour hot mixture over tomatoes.

Let stand for 4 days.

Separate tomatoes from syrup and cook syrup until it thickens.

Add tomatoes and bring to boil.

Put in sterile jars and seal.

Bread and Butter Pickles

    1 gallon med cucumbers (approx. 30)
    8 medium red, sliced onions
    2 large bell peppers – red, green or yellow
    ½ c. salt
    2 c. sugar
    3 c. apple cider vinegar
    2 T mustard seed
    1 t. turmeric
    1 t. whole cloves

Thinly slice cucumbers. Do not peel.

Slice onions in thin rings.
Cut peppers in narrow strips.
Dissolve salt in water and pour over vegetables.

Let stand for 3 hours. Drain.

Combine sugar, spices and vinegar in pan. Bring to boil.
Add drained vegetables and heat to point of boiling.

Remove from heat. Do not boil.

Pack in sterilized hot jars and seal.

Pickled Red Beets

Combine in saucepan:
1/3 c. vinegar
¼ c. water
½ t. cinnamon
¼ t. salt
¼ t. cloves, ground

Drain 2 cups sliced, cooked beets reserving the fluid for the pickled eggs.

Heat water and vinegar mixture to boiling. Add the 2 cups beets. Cover and simmer for 5 min. Chill.

Pickled Eggs

1 c. juice from cooked and/or pickled beets
1 c. organic apple cider vinegar
1 bay leaf
2 t. pickling spices, your choice
½ t. salt
12 hard cooked eggs
1 sm. onion sliced and separated in rings

In a large glass bowl or gallon jar combine all ingredients except eggs and onions. Stir. Add eggs and onion rings. Cover. Keep cool for several days.

Makes a dozen pickled eggs.

Hilde's German Potato Salad

Have ready:
6 c. sliced or diced and cooked potatoes, still warm. They need not be peeled.
Fry 16 slices bacon until crisp, approx. ¾ lb.
Reserve 2 T fat.
Crumble 12 slices over the potatoes.
Reserve 4 sliced for garnish.

Chop
1 small to medium sized onion
½ c. chopped celery
You will need:
2 T flour
1/3 c. vinegar
1/3 c. sugar
1/3 c. water
¼ t. pepper
1 t. chopped parsley

Fry chopped onion and celery in bacon fat until light brown. Reduce heat. Add flour and sugar until lumps disappear, then slowly pour in vinegar and water stirring continually until the mixture comes to boil.
Pour dressing over potatoes. Sprinkle with pepper, parsley, and either bacon curls or slices.
Serve hot.

Aunt Sadie's potato salad

5 – 6 large potatoes cooked in jackets until soft, then cooled, peeled and diced.
5 large hard-boiled eggs sliced
1 onion chopped
2 small grated carrots
1 c. diced celery
1 ½ t. salt
Mix ingredients in a large bowl.

Dressing:
½ T. corn starch
2 eggs
½ c. brown sugar
½ c. cider vinegar
1 t. mustard seeds
1 ½ c. water
2 T. butter

Mix dry ingredients. Stir in eggs, vinegar and water.
Melt butter in a saucepan, add other ingredients.
Cook until thickened.

Cool and pour over potato mixture.

Garnish with bread and butter pickles or salsa.

Autumn's Potato Salad

Mix together in a large bowl:
8 small red potatoes cooked and diced but not peeled.
1 c. chopped celery
¼ c. chopped onion
4 hard cooked eggs, peeled and sliced

Sprinkle over this mixture:
1 t. celery seed
1 t. mustard seed
1 t. Redmond sea salt
¼ c. extra virgin olive oil, cold pressed
1 T. organic vinegar
1 t. local honey

Cover and refrigerate until ready to serve.

Add ½ c. plain Greek yogurt. Stir.
Sprinkle with paprika and serve.

Optional: Garnish with fresh bell pepper slices, cherry tomatoes, parsley, or cucumbers in season for variety.

Please note: Autumn usually tasted and varied her recipes as she put them together.

Build That Wall

Tentative title and beginning of the sequel:

The Amish Time Traveler, book three

Rumm… Rumm… Rumm…
Conrad drove a tractor through the flower garden and ran into her tree.

Rumm… Rumm…
The noise got louder and louder
"Stay away," Kay screamed. "Don't hurt my babies!
Kay stood in front of the twins and spread her arms but the engine rattled on. A machine without a conscience.

Kay groaned awake and pulled the pillow over her head to drown the noise.
It puffed lower as if it were working harder. Then stopped…
"Want me to put in the post now?" Harley's voice sounded up through the house.
Kay scuttled to the bedroom window and stared at the scene below.
The rickety fence had been pulled out…. Completely and totally! No sign of it remained.
Harley and Levi had installed 20 or 30 feet of a chain link barrier. None of her neighbor's dogs would get out of her yard now.
Kay remembered the Amish way. If something needed fixing then do it.
If the neighbor's fence leaned on your property an English person would argue over the boundary but her family had lived a

simple life. They saved enough money to put up a fence for their neighbor without asking for anything in return.

In Amish socialism individual rights were not as sharply honed. Church members strove to live in peace under the Ordnung or rules for life.

Kay raised the screen and stuck her head out of the window. The rest of the sturdy materials for their project lay on the ground ready to go. The fence would last for years.

Levi must have asked the widow Miller if he could finish chores that her no-good son had managed to mess up.

"Knock. Knock." Autumn cracked open the door. "I come bearing coffee. Your children let me in."

Kay patted the bed next to her and sat with her back to the headboard. "I feel like royalty... sitting here while you wait on me."

"Harley told me he left Ohio in a hurry because Grandma B warned you to get the children away before Conrad came. What happened?"

"Harley took with my rental car minutes before Conrad got there with the local cop and a warrant for the immediate return of the twins. The policeman seemed embarrassed," Kay said. "He suggested that Levi might want to fix Conrad's brand new BMW because the battery cables seemed too tight."

Autumn laughed out loud.

"I miss those passive aggressive Dutchmen," she said. "There's no such thing as a battery cable that's too tight but the Amish may not know it so they wouldn't be complicit."

She shook her head back and forth as if in admiration.

"Conrad tried to shame me into helping him but my family was great. They sent him out to the pasture with a pillow case to find a snipe," Kay said.

"Good old fashioned Pennsylvania Dutch trickery," Autumn said. "There are no snipes in Holmes County. I wonder that Conrad fell for it."

The Amish Time Traveler

"Then mother made enough coffee to keep the men up all night. Levi set Conrad up with money making schemes," Kay said. "I've never been so ashamed of my choice of an ex-husband in my life."

"At least he's an ex," Autumn said.

Kay remembered her first conversations with Conrad... the thrill of disobeying her parents... the longing for a large diamond. She'd imagined how she would shock her family by showing them how English she'd become. She'd never considered how her husband would prove to be a dumKopf.

"Life's what happens when we've made other plans," Autumn said.

"Like Grandma B claiming I'm pregnant," Kay tried to grasp the impact of this news. It still felt too strange.

"I've never known Grandma B to be wrong." Autumn leaned over and held Kay's hand. "How do you feel about having another child? It is Conrad's isn't it?"

"Yes and I'm confused!" Kay said. "Depressed. Overwhelmed."

She paused to let silence pass between them. "Levi asked me to marry him and let him be the father."

Kay looked down at her lap. She loved children. Some people had abortions. She couldn't do that...

But her thinking... it felt flawed. Numb with emotion.

"He had feelings for you from the day you were born," Autumn said.

"You knew!"

"Anyone with eyes could see it. I wasn't positive you'd leave the Amish," Autumn said.

"I couldn't give up the books. Education!"

"Is he still single?"

"Widower. He married a Mennonite widow and helped her raise two children. She died last winter and now he thinks this baby is a gift from God... a final chance to have his own family."

"Children born in a marriage belong to the father whether he's biological or not," Autumn said. "How do you feel about that?"

"I don't know." Kay tried to name what bothered her. "I don't feel like I'm in love… no excitement like with Conrad. Or even Steve."

"That may be good," Autumn said. "Do you feel anything for him?"

"Safe. He'll take care of me," Kay said. "But not the same safe as with Hilde and you. He says he won't try to tell me what to do, but I don't know… if I don't marry him Conrad will try to take his baby. I need to protect my child."

"Having Conrad's baby isn't a good way to start a marriage with Levi. How much sleep have you had lately?" Autumn said. "There's an old Native American theory that abused children develop a link of loss. They feel incomplete without the thrill of betrayal. Conrad's behavior and you lack of sleep may just be the most compelling reasons for you to even consider marrying Levi."

Kay remembered her first date with Conrad. He'd spun the car in the snow and scared her until she threw up.

And she'd known she could change him.

Levi didn't need a woman to fix him. But putting in a new fence that bordered her property without so much as mentioning it to the woman he wanted to marry….

That kind of thing had to stop. He needed to ask her opinion before he bought something and installed it on the border of her property.

At the old age of 36 she finally stood single and on her own.

About time.

"Thank you for being my friend." Kay grabbed Autumn's hand and squeezed."

"You look like you need some breakfast," Autumn said. "Why don't you get dressed and we'll go to my house for some grub?"

Kay looked out the window. Harley and Levi had half the fence finished already and the twins seemed to be excited about helping.

No one needed her just yet.

"Sure. Let's go."" She pulled a shirt over her pajamas and followed her cousin barefooted.